Dogsbody

By the same author

Fred in Situ
The Loose Screw
Mud in His Eye
Dead Game
The Reward Game
The Revenge Game
Fair Game
The Game
Cousin Once Removed
Sauce for the Pigeon
Pursuit of Arms
Silver City Scandal
The Executor
The Worried Widow
Adverse Report
Stray Shot
Dog in the Dark
Doghouse

A Brace of Skeet
Whose Dog Are You?
Let Us Pray
Home To Roost
In Camera
Snatch Crop
Give a Dog a Name
Cash and Carry
The Curse of the Cockers
Thin Air
Carriage of Justice
Mad Dogs and Scotsmen
Hook or Crook
Sting in the Tail
Sink or Swim
Bloodlines
Follow That Gun
Twice Bitten

A Shocking Affair

By Gerald Hammond (originally published under the
pseudonym Arthur Douglas):

The Goods
A Very Wrong Number

Last Rights
A Worm Turns

Writing as Dalby Holden:

Doldrum

Gerald Hammond

Dogsbody

A John Cunningham Mystery

MACMILLAN

First published 1999 by Macmillan
an imprint of Macmillan Publishers Ltd
25 Eccleston Place, London SW1W 9NF
Basingstoke and Oxford

Associated companies throughout the world

ISBN 0 333 75263 5

1 3 5 7 9 8 6 4 2

A CIP catalogue record for this book is available from
the British Library.

Phototypeset by Intype London Ltd
Printed and bound in Great Britain by
Mackays of Chatham plc, Chatham, Kent

Chapter One

'About six months ago,' Hannah said idly, 'I was walking some puppies on the Moss and I met that old Irishman, the man with the two Pomeranians, and he said, "Sure, we're having a worse winter this summer than the summer we had last winter." '

'Oh, we laugh, but there's often a lot of logic in what the Irish say,' Daffy commented. 'I bet you understood exactly what he meant.' Daffy has Irish blood in her. She pours scorn on the Irish but always defends them against criticism, real or implied, from others.

Hannah nodded sleepily. 'Of course I did. I was just thinking that he couldn't say it again the other way round.'

She had a point. The rain had blown past by midday, to be succeeded by a furious wind that howled across north-east Fife, penetrating the warmest garments, sucking the heat out of anyone venturing outdoors and generating thoughts about retirement to Florida or the Bahamas. The best that could be said about the weather was that the snow which had been forecast had not yet arrived. We had scrambled somehow through all the work of the kennels, finishing in the early darkness of the Scottish winter.

All the dogs had been fed and brushed and the runs cleaned. Those dogs not in quarantine had been walked. Those in training had at least been given some work in the big barn and as the principal trainer as well as the founder and senior partner in the business I had braved the Moss with the two who had field-trial engagements in the near future. A recent litter of springer pups had been checked over, fondled and settled.

It was our unwinding time of day, when custom decreed that drinks and decisions would be taken and triumphs and disasters discussed. Beth, my wife, was upstairs and supervising the bedtime preparations of Sam, our only child, but the others were gathering. Isobel, the third partner in the business, matronly in cardigan and pink spectacles, was accepting a gin and tonic (large but I had made it rather dilute because Isobel, though no alcoholic, when in the mood is inclined to look on the wine while it is any colour of the spectrum). Daffy and Hannah, the two kennel-maids, each nursed a glass of an innocuous and modestly priced white wine which I had found on a back shelf of the supermarket. And I had a pint glass holding the former contents of a can of the Guinness which the others kept telling me that I liked, because it was supposed to be good for me. It was a time for relaxing, for relishing the peace and security of an established business and a busy but uncomplicated lifestyle.

Henry, Isobel's husband, though not a member of the firm, often joined us on these occasions but he was away on business.

A prime objective of these sessions was to review the health and progress of the dogs. If Daffy had observed that Ash had developed an occasional limp, it would not do for Hannah to let him out for a run before Isobel (a qualified vet) had treated him; while if I noticed that Polly was becoming nervous I would not want her scolded until we had got to the root of the problem.

Despite the weather, there were no disasters to discuss that day. We had moved on from the inevitable minor hiccups to idle speculation about Holly's chances of a win in an imminent field trial, when Beth came downstairs. 'There's a red glow in the sky,' she said.

'The sun went down ages ago,' Daffy said.

'It's in the wrong direction,' Beth said. 'Eastish. I think somebody's got a serious fire. They'll have a job putting it out in this wind. Sam wants to stay in bed and read,' she added. Sam was allowed to come down and join us in his pyjamas, but he had recently discovered the joys of the less heavy adult reading. His days were filled with school and dogs, so bedtime was reading time.

Beth found a seat between the two kennelmaids and accepted a sherry. I was, as always, mildly surprised to notice again how Beth, though she must be ten years older than either of the kennelmaids, still managed to look younger than both. I put it down to the babyish effect of large eyes and a button nose. We were bringing Beth up to date with the few pieces of intelligence worth passing on, when we saw a vehicle's lights on the curtains and heard its wheels on the gravel.

'Who could this be?' Daffy asked the ceiling.

'A client, I hope,' Beth said.

'You're curious. You go,' Hannah told Daffy.

'It's your turn, Dogsbody,' Daffy retorted.

'It's always my turn,' Hannah grumbled. 'Actually, for once I think it really is. So if nobody's feeling sorry for me . . .?' She waited hopefully but it seemed that nobody was feeling sorrier for her than she was. We were all tired. Hannah, who had worked as hard as anybody, climbed painfully to her feet and hobbled out of the room. She reached the front door just as the bell chimed. We heard voices, one of them high-pitched and distressed.

I felt a stirring of apprehension. I can recognize the threshold of hysteria. As the only man present as well as the titular owner of the property, I got reluctantly to my feet as the door reopened.

The newcomers, it seemed, comprised a slightly windswept policewoman and another woman who at first I could not place. It took me several seconds to recognize Mrs Hill, a widow from a village several miles away and a regular client. For this, I may be forgiven. I had never before seen Mrs Hill in any state other than perfect grooming. But now her blue-rinsed hair, usually dressed, sprayed and disciplined into rigid perfection, had escaped from the restraint of lacquer and stood up in spikes, rather like those of the Statue of Liberty, showing dark grey roots. She wore no coat and her dress, of a lilac material that looked like silk to me but was probably synthetic, was bloodstained.

4

Even her figure, usually appearing to be tightly corseted, seemed to have spread. Her make-up was smeared and running. Dark smuts staining her face and clothes were explained by a smell of soot.

I had never liked Evelyn Hill much. When another client first introduced her to me, her manner had clearly been that of a chatelaine to a visiting tradesman and provoked me into downright rudeness. 'There was an Evelyn Hill in the Falkland Islands,' I told her. 'We had to yomp over it on the way to Port Stanley.' I paused and an imp of mischief impelled me on. 'That wasn't you, was it?' I enquired. She had shaken her head without troubling herself even to interpret the opinions of underlings and went on to engage my services.

Her usual manner was haughty to the point of arrogance, as if her inheritance of money from her late husband relieved her of the need to be polite to anybody. Here, though, was a very different lady. I tried to offer her my chair but she was too agitated to sit down.

'Oh, Mr Cunningham,' she bleated, 'Atilla's hurt. Somebody kicked him or ran over him. I hoped . . . Mrs Kitts . . .'

'Yes. Of course,' Isobel said, getting to her feet.

'He's in the car.'

We hurried outside, staggering in the violence of the wind. Atilla was a large German shepherd. Mrs Hill, who lived alone except when one of her succession of housekeepers agreed to live in, had acquired him for a guard dog and brought him to me for training. In general, I like German shepherds and

Atilla was certainly a handsome beast with rather too friendly a nature for his calling, but he had proved to be as thick as porridge. At first he seemed unable even to recognize his own name or to realize that those noises uttered by humans were intended to convey any sort of message or command to him. With great patience, and at even greater expense to Mrs Hill, I had taught him those lessons and even introduced him to the basic elements of obedience. It was enough. He and his mistress adored one another. Fortunately he had just enough sense of territory to defend the house against intruders. I gathered that he had to be locked up when visitors were expected.

Atilla was undoubtedly in a bad way. There was blood in his mouth and at his back legs. He was in too much pain to move himself although at the sound of his mistress's voice his tail tried to twitch. To do her justice, Mrs Hill had tried her best. Her soft tweed coat was wrapped around the dog and, when Isobel had given Atilla a tranquillizing and painkilling injection, we used the coat to carry him into the tiny surgery where Isobel attends to any ailments among our stock and to a few clients who insist on coming to her for veterinary help.

Daffy, who often acts as Isobel's assistant and nurse, shooed the rest of us out. We returned to the sitting room and I coaxed Mrs Hill into a chair.

Beth and Hannah were frothing with questions but I hurried to get what I considered to be the important one in first. 'You'll be in need of a drink?' I asked her.

She seemed to be too dazed to answer. The WPC, who had settled neatly into an upright chair outside the main grouping, caught my eye. She indicated Mrs Hill, mouthed the word 'Brandy' and made a gesture indicative of large size. I had been thinking along the same lines. I poured out a stiff one, topped up the other glasses and looked at the WPC.

'How about you?' I asked. 'We won't tell.'

'My breath might,' she said. 'But vodka and tonic don't give you away. A small one, please.'

As I poured, I asked, 'What on earth happened?'

Mrs Hill took a long pull at her brandy, swallowed, shuddered in a ladylike manner and pulled herself at least partly together. 'I don't *know* what happened,' she said. 'There was a fire . . .'

'Perhaps you'd better tell it from the beginning,' the WPC said. When I took her drink to her, I saw that she had out her occurrence book and was writing in it on her knee. I wondered whether some good friend should not warn Mrs Hill against saying anything that she would not want quoted in court. I decided that I was not her good friend, that she had probably done nothing to be ashamed of and that if she had indeed sinned she deserved whatever was coming to her.

Mrs Hill drank again. 'All I know is that I was coming home—'

'From?' the WPC asked softly.

'I'd been in Dundee, at the shops, and I was late getting home. Traffic on the bridge was slow, because of this awful wind. They were sending lorries over in pairs. When I was still miles away, I could see the glow in the sky.'

Beth jumped and nearly spilled her sherry. 'We

could see a glow from here,' she said. 'Was . . . is that Atherton House?'

Mrs Hill began simultaneously to sob and nod. It took some minutes to soothe her with brandy and tissues. I had time partially to revise my opinion of her. She had evinced more immediate concern for her dog than for her property, which showed more humanity than I had previously given her credit for. As I remembered it, Atherton House was, or perhaps had been, a handsome house, at least when glimpsed from the road in passing, very much in the Scottish vernacular as envisaged by the disciples of Queen Victoria, all crow-stepped gables and unexpected turrets. It was the last house in its village and from its own wooded grounds it overlooked farmland. I had been told that the interior was furnished with equally handsome antiques and housed a valuable collection of china. I decided that a modicum of hysteria was forgivable in the circumstances if not actually de rigueur.

By the time she had been brought back to coherence, Mrs Hill's face was streaked with a jumble of assorted cosmetics. Her nose in particular had been blown on a tissue which had already been used to wipe mascara-laden eyes. I would dearly have loved to photograph her. But she was game to struggle on.

'There were two fire engines there already,' she said. 'Some neighbours had phoned. I was stopped at the bottom of the drive. The whole place was ablaze. Flames were coming out of the windows and the roof was smoking. I don't think they saved anything. I . . . I was trying to find out more when somebody told me about Atilla. From what they said, he was lying near the front door when the first engine arrived and they nearly ran over him. Well, there wasn't anything I could do there so my first thought was to get Atilla to the vet. I gave them my coat and they brought him out to me. I hope . . . do you think Mrs Kitts can save him?' The unanswerable question seemed to be aimed at me.

'She'll do everything possible,' I assured her.

'I seem to have lost everything else,' she said.

The floodgates were about to open again so I hurried to intervene. 'I'm sure it's not as bad as that,' I said. 'You still have your beautiful car. Your money's safe in the bank or invested.' A horrid thought came to me uninvited. 'You didn't keep it sewn into the mattress?'

She shook her head and even managed the ghost of a smile. 'I'm not a complete fool,' she assured us.

'Your insurance is up to date?'

'Revised and renewed a few months ago, thank God,' she said. 'The insurance agent came to look the place over. I think he was checking to see that I really did have all the valuables I said I had,' she finished indignantly. Out of the corner of my eye I could see the WPC, head down and writing.

'You'll still own the site and gardens if you want to rebuild,' I pointed out. 'Your insurance can't cover sentimental value, but it can provide for replacements. It could all have been very much worse.'

She heaved a shuddering sigh. 'You're right,' she said. 'I must pull myself together.' Her face fell. 'But what am I going to *do-oo?*'

'Take it a step at a time,' I told her.

She seemed ready to succumb to the vapours again. This time it was the WPC who headed her off. 'Are you sure that there would have been nobody in the house?' she asked.

Mrs Hill forgot to be sorry for herself for a moment. She frowned. 'There must have been an intruder,' she began. 'The wiring was perfect. I'd had it checked this year.'

'What about your housekeeper?' Beth asked. 'Elsie Bland, isn't it?'

'Oh.' There was a pause. I gathered that Mrs Hill had forgotten the existence of her housekeeper. 'No. Miss Bland has the afternoons off. She usually goes to visit her sister in Balcraigs. I told the other policeman that.' Mrs Hill broke off. The mind often takes refuge in irrelevancies in times of crisis. 'Is it all right to say "the other policeman"?' she asked the WPC. 'Or should I say "policeperson"?'

The WPC half-smiled. 'We won't worry too much about political correctness,' she said. 'Go on about Miss Bland.'

Mrs Hill brought her mind back. 'Miss Bland has a motor scooter. Usually she gets back in time to make me an evening meal – I dine late, I don't like to go to bed on an empty stomach – and if she plans to be later than that she leaves me a meal ready to heat up in the microwave or the oven, with all the instructions written down, because I was never much of a cook. But I suppose I should have said all that in the past tense,' she said drearily. 'She won't be doing it any longer.'

'She won't?' said the WPC alertly.

'How can she? The house isn't there any more.'

The WPC subsided.

'You'll have another house and maybe she'll come with you,' Beth said comfortingly.

'She wouldn't have gone off on her scooter in this wind,' Hannah pointed out. 'She'd have been blown off it in the first mile.'

'I'm sorry to have to tell you this at such a time,' said the WPC, 'but you have to know. Miss Bland is not accounted for. An officer has been to Balcraigs but nobody knows of a sister. And there seem to be the remains of a motor scooter in what's left of your garage.'

'But how extraordinary!' Mrs Hill looked totally bemused. What the lady's next reaction to the news would have been we never knew because Isobel had appeared in the door with Daffy behind her. 'And I'm sorry to bring more bad news,' Isobel said, 'but we lost him. The damage was just too severe. If it's any help or comfort, my opinion is that he wasn't kicked but run over. And not by anything as heavy as a fire engine.'

The succession of blows seemed almost too much for Mrs Hill to bear. She swallowed the last of her drink – her third or fourth, I thought – and leaned back with her eyes closed.

'Would you like us to call your doctor?' Beth asked. 'He could give you something . . .'

Mrs Hill, without opening her eyes, shook her head.

The WPC was restless. No doubt she was overdue to go off duty but she could hardly leave Mrs Hill, in a mentally shattered state, adrift in a hostile world.

11

'Do you have any relatives who could look after you?' she asked.

'Nobody,' Mrs Hill said plaintively. 'I have a cousin in Edinburgh but he's a busy man and he lives alone in a tiny apartment. He's an accountant, you know,' she added with a touch of vicarious pride. 'Chartered, of course.'

'Shall I take you to the hotel?'

Mrs Hill's eyes snapped open. 'Please, I couldn't bear to be among strangers.'

'Or friends?' asked the WPC.

'Not that I could ask, not really. Only . . .'

The lady's eyes seemed to be wandering round without guidance on her part, but I knew what she meant. And the last thing I wanted was to be saddled with a demanding and unattractive woman for an indefinite period. It was not as if we could even expect her to help with the chores. And bedroom space was always at a premium.

I tried to send Beth a warning look, but she was too quick for me. 'Of course you can stay here,' she said. 'Only . . .'

I knew what that *only* meant. Only Sam would have to sleep in the sitting room. Only we would have to sit in the kitchen of an evening if we wanted any privacy. Only we would have Mrs Hill across the landing from us and sharing our bathroom.

'Oh, could I?' breathed Mrs Hill.

'If it would help, I could go home for the night,' Hannah said. She owned a smart sports car and was always looking for excuses to use it. We brightened.

Hannah occupied a small extension at the back of the house, with tiny bathroom en suite.

'Listen,' Daffy said. We listened. The wind was as loud as ever. 'They've probably closed the bridge by now. You can come to me, Hannah. Just as long as you've gone before Rex comes back from offshore next week.' Daffy and her oil-worker husband occupied a cottage in the nearby village.

'That's settled, then,' said the WPC with evident relief. 'I'll come back tomorrow for a statement.' She had arrived as a passenger in Mrs Hill's car. She carried her radio outside to ask for transport to collect her.

By now, Mrs Hill not only looked like something abandoned when the circus left town, she was also stunned by an excess of emotion and brandy. None of us felt like having her underfoot so we conspired to dispose of her. While Daffy took Isobel home in my car and collected a nightdress of possibly adequate girth for the visitor, I shot another brandy into the lady. Beth and Hannah prepared Hannah's room and then put the exhausted Mrs Hill to bed in it while Daffy and I made a start to the preparation of our belated evening meal. Almost as an afterthought, Beth put a glass of water and several paracetamols beside the bed.

As we shared the hastily prepared mixed grill, Beth said, 'I wonder if Elsie Bland's all right.' It was a good point and one which seemed to have been skirted.

Chapter Two

Most things, we are told, look brighter in the morning, but Mrs Hill proved to be an exception. I found her in the kitchen and tackling without enthusiasm a very small bowl of cornflakes when I returned with Haughty from the Moss. (Proper name Hawthorn, but he was a dog who thought that he knew it all and he had a way of looking at you as though you had lost your marbles, so the pet name stuck.) Mrs Hill was washed and tidied, her hair had been restored to a sort of order and she was dressed, after a fashion, in what I recognized as one of Beth's maternity dresses, put away after the birth of Sam in the vain hope that it might be called into service again. Mrs Hill, it was explained later, was shorter than Isobel or Daffy or Hannah and too full of figure for any of Beth's other clothes. But the implication that her stoutness was due to a late pregnancy seemed to be troubling her almost as much as her other woes.

If Mrs Hill was no longer windblown and smut- and bloodstained, she showed no improvement in other respects. Her face, despite lavish application of make-up, was mottled and swollen with weeping or plain bad temper. She also seemed to be distinctly hung over and, from the way that she blinked, I had the impression that she was seeing spots. In times of crisis, I tend to dispense alcohol with a heavy hand.

The wind had almost blown itself out but the remaining breeze had an arctic bite. The illness which had terminated my army career was more or less cured but I was still seriously underweight and so was inclined to feel the cold. All that I wanted in the world was a hot drink and a chair beside the kitchen range. I was in no mood to make conversation with a selfish and domineering widow. Nor did I have any great sympathy with her, at least over the loss of her home. Henry had known the Hills well.

Internally, he had told me, Atherton House, although beautifully furnished, had been a gloomy mausoleum of a place, at one time the seat of a minor landowner but long since separated from the farmland. The rules of courtesy, however, were drummed into me in my youth and I am too old to shake them off now. Moreover, anyone bereft of a much-loved dog could be sure of my sympathy, however undeserving of that love the dog may have seemed.

Mrs Hill had moved to one of the basket chairs beside the range. When I was seated with a large mug of coffee on the other, I asked her what the latest situation might be.

'Situation?' she said vaguely.

I bit back a tart remark. 'Has Miss Bland turned up?' I asked patiently.

She looked blank. 'I don't know,' she said. 'I expect so. Nobody's told me anything.' It was clear that she had again forgotten her housekeeper's existence. I had an uncomfortable feeling that if Miss Bland had returned safely to the house somebody would have been in touch with her employer, but there would have been nothing to be gained by worrying the lady. Not that Mrs Hill would have been more than mildly concerned, and that only for her own convenience, even if Miss Bland had combusted spontaneously before her eyes.

'I don't know what to do,' she said plaintively. It seemed that Miss Bland was already forgotten again.

I put my mug down on the mantel and fetched writing materials. 'It helps to make a list,' I told her, putting a pencil and paper into her hands.

'List?'

'Just make notes,' I said. 'You'll need clothes. You have your car and your chequebook and credit cards?'

'Yes.' She looked down and plucked at Beth's maternity dress. 'But I can't go into Dundee like this.'

Beth had been flitting in and out of the kitchen, doing many simultaneous tasks as is her custom. She paused to join in the discussion. 'I'm afraid you're going to have to,' she said. 'The dress you were wearing yesterday might clean but it certainly won't wash.'

The idea that others might have more to do than dance attendance on her seemed to be foreign to Mrs Hill. 'If I gave you my size, couldn't you go and shop for me?'

'No, I couldn't,' Beth said shortly. 'You really have to try things on or they don't fit properly. The nominal sizes aren't more than a guide. And I wouldn't have any idea of your taste.' I gathered that she was already regretting the compassionate impulse that had prompted her to issue the invitation.

A change of subject was called for. 'You must notify your insurers,' I reminded her. 'And your cousin. If anything's happened to Miss Bland, I suppose you can count on the police to notify her sister when they find her. And you'll have to look around for somewhere to live. You'll have to decide whether you want to rebuild or buy again. Whichever you decide, you'd better rent somewhere furnished for the moment.'

She wrote down my words but without seeming to take them in. 'I've never had to do anything like that,' she said, still plaintive and wearing much the same expression as an overweight spaniel which can't understand why its dinner has been drastically reduced. 'Bob, my husband, used to do all that sort of thing.' She looked at me hopefully. Evidently I was expected to step into Bob's shoes at least so far as would suffice to save her from having to think for herself or take positive action.

'We can put you in touch with a good solicitor, if you don't have one of your own,' Beth said quickly. 'He could see to all that for you. And perhaps you should think about a hotel until you get organized.'

The notion seemed to horrify her. 'But I'd be among strangers.'

I was on the point of telling her that we were not exactly friends but Beth decided to postpone that piece of news until Mrs Hill had the reassurance of new and more suitable clothing to bolster her confidence. 'You'll have to do something about Atilla,' Beth said.

Mrs Hill was reminded of what was probably her

only unselfish reaction to the disaster. Her eyes filled with tears. 'My poor old boy!' she said. 'Mr Cunningham, you have a pets' cemetery here, don't you?'

'Not as such,' I said. 'We usually find homes for our retired stock, but sometimes they're brought back at the end of their days.'

'We like to feel that they're back where they were happy,' Beth said. 'And very occasionally a client has asked us to bury the ashes here. We have seven or eight graves in the back lawn, marked by no more than flat stones, set flush with the grass so that the mower can go straight over the top of them.'

'Atilla was happy here,' Mrs Hill said. This was untrue. On the frequent occasions when his mistress took a holiday abroad, Atilla was usually left with us. I had originally given him the name and very suitable it had turned out to be. He had been friendly enough in his half-witted way while he was with us for basic training, but after prolonged spoiling at Atherton House he had found our kennels and runs less than what he felt to be his entitlement. A German shepherd, when less than gruntled, has ways of making its displeasure felt. The girls had retaliated by feeding him at long range and walking him hardly at all.

'Surely the garden at Atherton House would be more suitable,' I suggested. 'But it isn't urgent quite yet. Think about it.' Beth looked at me curiously.

While we were discussing the disposal of the unfortunate Atilla I had thought of several other duties which, left to herself, Mrs Hill would have forgotten or neglected in the hope that somebody else would undertake them for her. Before I could add to her list, however, there was the sound of an engine and the shadow of a large vehicle partially dimmed the kitchen for a moment.

'I'll see who it is,' Beth said. 'You two carry on.'

The very idea of 'carrying on' with Mrs Hill took my breath away. By the time I had dictated one or two items for the list, Beth had returned, bringing with her the WPC from the previous evening, followed by the familiar and burly figure of Detective Inspector Burrard. The Inspector's rosy face, like Beth's, always reminded me of a baby's although in his case not a very pretty one. He was comparatively inexperienced in CID work but I had never found him short of mature intelligence. His habit of being driven and assisted by the younger and more attractive uniformed WPCs did nothing to lower my opinion of him.

It was obvious to me that Burrard would not have been present for an accidental fire without loss of life. 'You want to see Mrs Hill?' I suggested. 'You'd better go through to the sitting room.'

Mrs Hill would not have recognized the Detective Inspector but she must have read something into the visitors' body language. I saw her stiffen and she gripped the arms of the basket chair until they creaked in protest. 'I'd rather stay here,' she said. It was a plea for support.

'People will be in and out of here all morning,' I told her. 'This kitchen gets like Sauchiehall Street at times.' I hesitated. There were ten thousand tasks awaiting me. 'But I'll come with you, if you wish,' I added reluctantly.

'I'd be very grateful.' (This was another untruth. Mrs Hill was never grateful for anything. Beth suggested later that it might be against her religion.)

I led the way across the hall. The sitting room is rather deep for its window and always seems gloomy on a dull day. Also, the central heating, for some reason which had baffled a series of heating engineers, always left that room to last before shrugging off the overnight chill. But there were remedies available. I switched on some subdued lighting. Two firelighters and a few logs soon had a fire burning above the ashes of the previous evening. Suddenly the room was cosy and, I hoped, reassuring.

The inspector wore a similarly comforting face. He enquired after her health and asked how she was recovering from the shock of the previous day's events. Reassured by these overtures, the widow became almost flirtatious and, suddenly calling to mind what would be expected of her, asked, without any great show of interest in the answer, whether there was any news of Miss Bland.

Immediately, Burrard looked respectfully solemn. 'That's why we're here,' he said. 'The aftermath of the fire only became cool enough to examine at an early hour of the morning and it wasn't pronounced safe to enter until little over an hour ago. As soon as they began to move the debris a human body was found in the shell of the kitchen. The police surgeon was of the opinion that the body was female.'

Mrs Hill's first thought, as always, was for herself. 'I do hope,' she began, 'that you aren't going to ask me to—'

'Nothing like that,' the Inspector assured her quickly.

'They'll ask the sister,' I said. 'Close relatives are always preferred.'

'Well now,' said Burrard. 'That brings me to the nub of what I wanted to discuss. But, first, can you tell me what dentist and doctor Miss Bland attended? And her bank, if you know it.'

It must have been as obvious to Mrs Hill as it was to me that such interest in Miss Bland's medical attendants meant that the body was burned beyond visual identification. She turned white and clamped her hands together, but she gave the required information in a subdued voice. Miss Bland had registered, on Mrs Hill's recommendation, with the latter's doctor and dentist. The WPC, sitting as before outside the group of participants, received a nod and slipped out of the room.

'Last night,' said Burrard, 'you told two separate officers that Miss Bland was in the habit of spending her afternoons with her sister in Balcraigs. Would that have been a married sister?'

'I . . . I assumed so,' Mrs Hill said. 'I never thought to ask her. Why would I?'

The DI ignored her question as rhetorical. 'There are no Blands living in or near Balcraigs – which is, after all, only a small village where everybody knows everybody else. Nor have we found a trace of any lady with that for a maiden name.'

'I'm only going by what she told me,' Mrs Hill said defensively.

'You never met this sister?'

Mrs Hill bridled slightly. 'Certainly not.'

'And you're sure that she said "in Balcraigs"? Those words?'

'Oh dear! I can't say that I was paying any particular attention. She certainly mentioned Balcraigs. I thought she said "in" but she might have said "near". Or she might have said that she had to go through Balcraigs to get there.'

'That last would hardly be likely. There's very little beyond Balcraigs except Tentsmuir Forest and the North Sea. Could she have said "in the direction of Balcraigs"?'

'I suppose she must have done,' said Mrs Hill doubtfully. 'There's no other explanation, is there?'

Detective Inspector Burrard was saved from having either to answer or evade the question by the return of the WPC, presumably having passed on the information about Miss Bland's doctor and dentist. 'You may note down,' Burrard told her, 'that Mrs Hill is still sure that Miss Bland mentioned Balcraigs but is uncertain whether she said "in" or "near" or "on the way to" or even "on the other side of". Is that a fair summary?' he asked.

Mrs Hill nodded.

'Answer aloud, please, for the record.'

'Yes,' said Mrs Hill. The WPC wrote the word down.

Gently but firmly, Burrard continued with questions, but without much profit. Mrs Hill had a clear recollection of where she had been all day, but she had flitted from shop to shop without making any substantial purchases and there were unlikely to be any witnesses to her whereabouts for most of the afternoon. No, she would not have expected to know that her housekeeper had decided not to go out that after-noon. And—

'No,' she said firmly, drawing herself up with as much dignity as can be assumed by a stout lady seated in a deep armchair, 'as far as I know neither Miss Bland nor I had any enemies. I knew comparatively little about her, but as far as I am concerned . . .' She seemed about to suggest that she was beloved by all but she was sidetracked by another thought. 'What is the purpose of that question?' She stared at him, faint but determined.

Burrard caught my eye. If it had been in his mind to retort that he would ask the questions, thank you very much, he must have realized that I would immediately have advised the lady to stop answer-ing them. 'Enquiries have only just begun,' he said. 'But the preliminary opinion of the Brigade's Fire In-vestigator is that the fire may have been started deliberately. And the police surgeon reported a depressed fracture in the back of the body's skull. Post-mortem examination will surely determine whether that injury was caused before death or by the collapse of the structure in the fire. And we await a final report on the cause of the fire. Meantime, until we can be sure that the fire and the death were both accidental, you must surely see that we have to gather up evi-dence that may otherwise become lost.'

Mrs Hill looked at me helplessly.

'That seems quite reasonable,' I told her. 'Of course, you'd be quite entitled to have a solicitor present – ' she shook her head – 'but if you're relying on my advice I can only say that, from what little I know, it seems to me that you should answer the Inspector's questions.'

Burrard looked pleased but it turned out that he only had a few more questions to ask, none of which Mrs Hill was able to answer, and those were of a routine nature such as the make of Miss Bland's scooter. 'I think that's all for the moment,' he said. 'I take it that if I want you again you'll be here?' He caught my eye. 'Or that you'll notify us of any change of address?' he added quickly.

'Definitely. And is it all right for us to bury the dog?' I asked.

'I'll let you know after I've seen Mrs Kitts.'

'She went into Cupar with Hannah,' I said, 'but I heard the car come back. I'll see if she's in the house.'

'And I can go and buy some clothes and things,' Mrs Hill said more cheerfully.

I found Isobel in her tiny surgery, putting away the veterinary supplies that had been the object of her journey. The corpse of Atilla still lay on the table, covered by a cloth. I spared a thought for the late lamented. He had been unusually dim for a German shepherd and distinctly cranky, but he had been beautiful.

I had hoped to go away and do something useful, but Isobel asked me to be with her. 'I like to have a witness to what I do and don't say,' she explained. 'Henry taught me that.'

The Detective Inspector showed no surprise and raised no objection when I returned with Isobel and resumed my chair. There was no sign of Mrs Hill.

'Yesterday,' he said, 'you were of the opinion that the dog had been knocked down by a vehicle rather than kicked or struck with a weapon.'

'I still am,' said Isobel. 'The injuries were typical. Not localized but spread over the central part of the body. Most of the major organs were damaged by crushing.'

'And none of the injuries suggested an attack? What I'm getting at is that the dog might have been struck down with a blunt weapon first and then run over.'

'I didn't see anything of the sort. But I was concerned with trying to save the dog's life, not determining the causes of his injuries.'

Detective Inspector Burrard cogitated for some seconds. 'I see,' he said at last. 'I could have the body sent to the Divisional Veterinary Officer for a post-mortem examination, but that would take time and might be distressing for Mrs Hill. Would you be able to carry it out?'

'I've done a dozen autopsies on dogs and cats. Not for the police,' Isobel explained, 'but for distressed owners who wanted to know, for their peace of mind, what the little darling had died of. I could carry out a physical examination and record my findings.'

'And take samples for laboratory examination,' said Burrard, 'just in case the dog was doped, which would be one possible explanation of his lying in the drive, waiting for a vehicle to run over him.'

'I'll get onto it straight away.'

'No, don't do that. I'll send a technician first, to get

what traces he can from the dog's pelt. You never know.'

'All right, Inspector,' Isobel said. 'But do it quickly. I don't want an outsize corpse going past its bury-by date in my surgery any longer than strictly necessary.'

'If I can,' said Burrard. 'It may depend on avail-ability. After that . . . Bury the dog, by all means, but no cremation, not yet. Something may turn up which suggests further examination.' He smiled, faintly but consolingly. 'I can't for the life of me think what, but I do like to anticipate.'

Money may not bring happiness but it can certainly help to solve a lot of problems. Mrs Hill had been balking at the idea of going to Dundee in Beth's old maternity dress in order to start replacing her lost wardrobe. What kind of clothes, she wondered aloud, would she be offered if she entered the better shops looking like one who had been ejected from a tinker's encampment for letting down the sartorial image? She was saved from that fate by the sudden recollection that two of her favourite dresses were by then awaiting collection from the cleaners in Cupar. When each member of the firm had declined to go and fetch them for her on the grounds of pressure of work, she even-tually solved the problem for herself. One phone call to the cleaners and another to a taxi firm and she was in a position to dress in a manner which she con-sidered appropriate. She had no coat other than the one stained with Atilla's blood but she decided that she could stand the cold for the length of pavement between the car park and the nearest shop of passable quality. She took herself off quite cheerfully in her shining Audi.

The middle of the day was filled with the routine of the kennels. The threatened snow had passed us by. I loaded sandwiches, a thermos flask and several dogs into the car and took them off to my favourite farm with the intention of steadying the dogs to live game and rabbits. Hannah and Daffy and Beth cleaned and brushed and walked and fed and fondled our residents and checked them for parasites and for damage or gorse prickles in the tails of those which, thanks to the combined idiocies of Parliament and the RCVS, still had the full appendage. Between times, the domestic chores were done, mostly by Beth.

The sun was already low in the sky when I got back to Three Oaks and the old farmhouse glowed against the darkening landscape. I delivered my charges to Daffy, who examined them carefully in case I had allowed any of them to injure themselves or roll in something disgusting. I walked round the house to fetch a spade and dig a last resting place for Atilla. But one of the girls – Hannah, I learned later – had anticipated me and there was a neat rectangular hole just where I had planned to put it. My health was still uncertain and those around me conspired to spare me any heavy physical labour, whenever they remembered.

Isobel had finished. I found her at the kitchen table, which gave her more space than the desk in the tiny office – for writing, I mean, not the autopsy. She was drafting her report, but she gave me the gist of it while I prepared for myself a mug of hot soup (from a packet). She had found little new, and nothing to change her opinion that all Atilla's injuries had been caused by a vehicle. 'There was one other thing,' she added. 'I found a few small threads between his teeth. Of course, he may have been chewing at his bed or an old slipper, but they could be significant. I've put them in an envelope, for the Inspector. I suppose he could have bitten some visitor.'

'A visitor who then went bananas and burnt the place down, killing Atilla and Miss Bland in the process? Is that what you mean? That seems a bit drastic. And surely Mrs Hill would have locked the dog in the house when she went out, rather than leave him free to roam.'

Isobel shrugged. 'So maybe the visitor had a key,' she said. 'Or broke in.'

Out of pure curiosity, I was about to ask her whether she could make a guess as to whether the vehicle had been heavy or light, but Sam arrived home from school. We were always careful to avoid topics in his presence which might give him nightmares or arouse morbid curiosity. But Mrs Hill returned almost on his heels and conscripted Sam to help her carry a baggage-train of packages up the stairs to Hannah's room. One of her few redeeming virtues was a fondness for the child. By the time the transportation was finished Sam had most of the story and was insisting that a 'proper' funeral must be carried out forthwith.

There was still enough light for the purpose

although shadows had already stretched across the garden and the last of the crows had gone to roost. No coffin was deemed necessary. Instead, Mrs Hill made permanent the sacrifice of her bloodstained tweed coat, on the grounds that Atilla would feel at home with it and that she couldn't wear the coat again anyway, and the body was laid to rest wrapped in it. Sam was allowed to conduct the service, which encompassed most of the full ritual from the Prayer Book.

Mrs Hill, at her most irritating, joined us uninvited at the drinks and debriefing which ended our working day. Instead of allowing our discussion to digest the events of the day and agree our plans for the immediate future, she monopolized the floor with a demand for the right to erect a headstone over the grave. This, I pointed out, was unacceptable. This was our lawn. None of the other graves was marked by more than a flat stone set flush with the grass so that it could be ignored by anyone steering the mower. If she cared to accept this less obstructive monument to her late pet we could find a suitable stone and set it in place. And there would be no need for a monumental mason to attend; Atilla's name was composed entirely of straight lines which the local builder could inscribe with his rotary cutting disc at far less cost. I allowed her to understand that if she was determined on a more upright memorial she could exhume her old friend and bury him somewhere else.

Mrs Hill accepted my edict, but not without

unblushingly accusing me of being insensitive, inflexible and autocratic.

The whole discussion, however, soon turned out to be, at least in the short term, academic . . .

Chapter Three

In the interests of my uncertain health, it is the custom of the house to let me sleep until I wake of my own accord. Sometimes I may be the first out of bed. More often I wake up to find that the day's work is well launched. On the morning after Atilla's interment I woke, as so often, to find myself alone in the bed. But the noises downstairs were not the compound of cheerful voices, trolley wheels and rattling feed dishes that I was used to. The voices were there, pitched at that annoying level just below the point at which words can be made out, but I could detect puzzlement and concern in the tones.

Some disaster had to have occurred to one of the dogs.

Without pausing to wash or dress, I donned a thick dressing gown and slippers and hurried downstairs. Beth, Isobel and Daffy were gathered in the kitchen, each of them looking baffled.

'What's the matter?' I asked. 'Something wrong with a dog?'

'Not in the way you mean,' said Beth. 'Now, you're not to get all het up—'

'But what's *wrong?*' I broke in.

She must have decided that I would get less 'het up' if told the truth than if kept in the dark. 'Nothing serious,' she said. 'Strange, even weird, but not serious. I just don't know whether it's something we should tell Mr Burrard about.' And before I had time to express my mounting frustration, she went on suddenly, 'Somebody's dug up Atilla and gone off with his remains. Daffy took some pups round that way this morning and there was a dashed great hole in the lawn where we buried Atilla yesterday.'

As soon as I had put on clothing suitable for going outdoors in Scotland in wintertime I went to see for myself, but it was a wasted journey. All was as Beth had already told me. There was a hole in the lawn where Atilla had been laid to rest – indeed, everything was much as it had been before the funeral except that Hannah had heaped the excavated earth neatly on an old tarpaulin whereas it was now dumped unceremoniously all over the grass. There were some blurred footprints to be seen in the displaced soil and the marks of a spade. The marks did not look very informative but I covered them with the old tarpaulin anyway, in case the threatening rain should come and wash them away.

Back in the kitchen, Beth had my breakfast ready. Why a sudden outbreak of dog'sbodysnatching should have given me an appetite I have no idea, but I attacked the bacon, egg and mushrooms eagerly and even managed to finish the dish and go on to toast and marmalade. Beth was pleased. I usually stall halfway through a small plate of cornflakes.

Daffy had gone off to help Hannah with the chores. Isobel and Beth were waiting to discuss the new development but Mrs Hill, beautifully dressed once again, carefully made-up and, to my eye, seriously ugly, put in an appearance and had to be apprised of the disappearance of her late friend. She was shocked and puzzled, but neither too shocked nor too puzzled to expect and accept a breakfast at least the match of mine. As a result, our participation in the first part of the discussion was muffled.

'I can't think who would want to do such a thing,' Beth said, not for the first time.

'Or why,' Isobel added. I had to agree. There is no ready market for dead dogs in this country and Atilla's pelt would hardly have made even a useful hearthrug.

I more or less emptied my mouth. 'You couldn't have missed anything that might incriminate somebody?' I asked her.

'Like what?'

'Damned if I know,' I said after a minute's thought. A dog may carry a thousand clues as to where it has been, what it has been doing and how it has been treated but it was difficult to see how any such information could have endangered the arsonist and killer.

'I didn't miss a damn thing,' Isobel said grumpily. 'I've done enough autopsies, God knows. Somebody's pet snuffs it from a surfeit of chocolate creams and they immediately want to know who poisoned the little ber – beggar. I usually tell them that it was cancer of the lymphatic gland, or something equally stupid, and nobody's fault. Then I try to steer them away from ever having another dog.'

Mrs Hill started to speak, paused for a quick swallow and went on. 'I suppose they wouldn't intend to ask for a ransom?' she suggested.

Beth looked doubtful. 'Would you pay a ransom for a dead dog?'

Mrs Hill halted the fork which had been on its way to her mouth. 'I didn't say I'd pay it,' she pointed out seriously. 'But that doesn't mean that they mightn't ask for it.'

I pushed my plate away. 'Did you examine the stomach contents?' I asked Isobel.

'I kept them for the police. That's more or less routine. But I don't think Atilla had been drugged.'

'I wasn't thinking of drugs,' I said. 'I was thinking more of incriminating material. Suppose, for instance, that somebody had offered Atilla a tasty snack of something slightly exotic from his own sandwiches, like ostrich-meat, to distract him while the evil deed was done. That somebody might then have realized that the food would point back to him. A top-notch guard-dog wouldn't be distracted but . . .'

'That didn't happen,' said Mrs Hill sadly. 'Anyone who shared his sandwiches with Atilla would have made a friend for life. So he wouldn't have got run over by running round in front of the car and barking. He only did that with people he didn't like. You did your best, and Atilla was a wonderful companion, but as a watchdog the most you could say for him was that he barked a lot and sometimes bit strangers.'

'Definitely gut-oriented,' I agreed. 'Do the police

have the fibres from between his teeth? Maybe those will suggest something.'

We batted around a number of ideas of increasing improbability. 'There are two things to be done,' I said at last. 'And the first is to let the police know what's happened. There's no way that this could not be connected in some way to the fire. You could do that, Beth.'

'And what's the second thing?' Beth asked.

'I'm going to go and do it now,' I said. Beth left it at that. Neither of us likes to discuss ideas in embryo.

I wrapped myself up again and went in the direction of the kennels, but instead of taking out a spaniel or two for the usual endless training I fetched Jason. With the prospect of a walk, the old boy managed to frisk a little. Despite the strange happenings, I felt much as he did. The weather had relented. An early frost was melting on the grass, the sun had come out, geese were on the move against a sky that went on for ever and the world looked as though winter might some day end.

When we first set up in business we had a firm agreement that there would be no personal pets but that all dogs would be for breeding or training or sale. That held good for about a year. Then Jason arrived – Beth's personal Labrador, a legacy from an uncle. Beth had never quite managed to make him up to Field Trial Champion, but together they had earned several Certificates of Merit and in the process she had learned a great deal about handling dogs in competition and in the field. Jason was an old dog now, but he had always been possessed of a better nose than any spaniel and he had a strong sense of territory. I could count on him to tell me of the scent of a stranger.

We began to explore the land to the north of the house. My idea was a simple one. Somebody had known that Atilla was buried in the back lawn. It seemed probable that the funeral had been observed. But a watcher might have been deceived into believing that the forensic science technician who had come to collect traces from Atilla's thick pelt had removed the body, in which case he (or she) would not have stayed on and observed the funeral. The technician had backed his van up to the front door, to cut down the distance that he would have to carry his rather heavy vacuum cleaner. Only from certain angles could a watcher have seen that only the vacuum cleaner left the house. Or the case holding that device might have been mistaken for some sort of coffin. A casual watcher might not have waited to witness the funeral and so would not have known where to look for the departed.

Three Oaks is entirely surrounded by farmland. We began by investigating the hedges and hollows near the house and to its north. Any approach from the south by a stranger would have passed close to the kennels and would undoubtedly have set the dogs barking.

There were rabbits along the first hedge, or so Jason assured me, but no recent human traces. We moved further out, among the gorse bushes on the rising ground, trying to keep to an angle from which the technician's activities could have been seen. The garden was laid out like a map below us and we could see beyond to the village a mile away, sharp in the clear air. But here there were too many scents, of the farmer and his dogs and the sheep, and I could tell by Jason's rising hackles that a fox had passed that way. He paused to sniff at a hollow between two gorse bushes. His hackles stayed flat but we were far enough from the house that his sense of territory might have been in abeyance. I soon gave up and hurried back to the house with Jason trotting happily beside me. Well, at least he had enjoyed the outing. The brief period of morning sunshine was over and dark clouds were foaming up from the west.

Beth had phoned the police headquarters in Kirk-caldy and reported the theft of property, to wit one dead dog, to a member of the police who had seemed incredulous but had promised to pass the word along if only to give the Detective Inspector a laugh.

That reaction seemed to leave us free to get on with the business of the day. But first I looked for Mrs Hill and found her in the sitting room with her feet up in front of a log fire, reading a magazine. I took another chair. She blinked at me, coming slowly out of whatever world of fashion or romantic fiction the magazine had transported her to.

'Somebody knew where to look for Atilla,' I said. 'A casual visitor couldn't see the back lawn but I've found a place from where a really determined watcher could have observed the funeral. Nobody would have been watching from there without having some prior infor-mation. So who did you tell that Atilla was dead and that we were going to bury him here?'

She looked guilty. 'It wasn't a secret,' she said.

'No, of course it wasn't. Just unfortunate, as it turns out, but in a sense it's your loss more than ours. We'll have to tidy the grass but you've lost contact with your old friend.'

'Poor Atilla,' she said, but it was no more than a token lament. The memory of Atilla was fading already. 'I met some friends for lunch at the Angus Hotel. There were eight of us. Well, most of them knew that I had been burned out of house and home and they wanted to chat about the details. But you surely don't think that any of my friends—?'

'I don't suppose so for a minute. But if each of the other seven told three more people . . . Would they do that?'

'I . . . I don't know.'

'Then we can count on it,' I said.

By then, the rain had begun – fortunately not until after most of the dogs had had a morning walk. Most of a spaniel's training can only be given in the great outdoors, but there are certain lessons which can be taught under cover. Rather than bring back a succession of soaking and muddy spaniels for the others to cope with, I spent most of the day in the big barn, reinforcing basic obedience and hiding dummies in the straw before setting my various pupils problems and temptations suitable to the stage of education which each had attained. Soon I was absorbed. Atilla seemed to be far away, which, of course, he was.

The disadvantages of having Mrs Hill as a guest were not limited to the nature of the lady herself. She and

the events centred around her attracted the police to
Three Oaks like Labradors homing in on a discarded
sandwich. We were visited late that afternoon, not by
the Detective Inspector nor even by a detective
sergeant but by the uniformed WPC who had been
Burrard's companion (or possibly chaperone) the previous day. Paradoxically, this told me that the police
were taking the fire at Atherton House seriously – very
much more seriously than they were taking the theft
of a dead dog. On a routine matter, DI Burrard would
probably have done the follow-up himself; but when a
case is big and looks set to become bigger a growing
team is involved. The more senior members of that
team coordinate the investigation and interview
crucial witnesses or suspects. Lesser side issues are
delegated to officers with seniority proportionate to
the importance of the issues. I gathered that the
removal of Atilla's corpse was considered intriguing
rather than important. It had, after all, been stripped
of all its secrets.

Or so we thought.

The girls were busy but I told them to keep Sam
with them when he arrived home from school. I
showed the WPC the site of the outrage. The rain had
let up and the footprints still showed. She recognized
their possible usefulness immediately and used her
radio to request technical assistance in preserving
them. They were blurred and becoming more so, but
they might give an expert an indication as to the size
and weight of the culprit.

I brought her into the sitting room, by which time
Beth had kindled the fire and made a pot of tea. Mrs

Hill had been shopping again but had returned only minutes before the arrival of the WPC, whose name, we were to learn, was Cotton.

WPC Cotton was unable, or more probably unwilling, to divulge any information about the investigation into the fire and the body. She listened to the story while taking it down in shorthand. The WPC, now that I was able to study her away from the overpowering presence of the Detective Inspector, was an attractive young lady. The women's police uniform, although intended to be asexual, by its very severity lends emphasis to the femininity of the wearer. I found that my voice was tending towards an insinuating warmth when I addressed her. I saw Beth glance at me once or twice, so I was happy to let her and Mrs Hill tell most of the tale, for all that there was of it. WPC Cotton, I noticed, had acquired the difficult knack of taking down her own questions as well as the answers without interrupting the flow.

She listened to an account of the funeral and the robbery and then asked, 'Mrs Kitts had done a full autopsy and found nothing beyond the dog having been run over? And the technician had visited and vacuumed the dog's pelt?' We agreed. 'Then,' she went on, 'can you suggest what anybody might have to fear from the body or to gain by removing it?' She was well and almost pedantically spoken – a graduate of St Andrews, I discovered later.

'Whoever it was may not have known that any evidence on the dog had already been preserved,' I said, keeping my voice carefully neutral. 'I went round with a Labrador to find out if there were signs of

somebody watching the house and got little or no reaction, but that's hardly conclusive.'

WPC Cotton finished writing and looked up at me.
'A watcher could have been sitting in a car on the
road.'

'I was sure that there wasn't a car parked outside
the gates for any length of time,' I said, 'and anyone
watching from the road would have thought that your
technician had removed the whole body in his van –
in which case he wouldn't have waited around long
enough to see the funeral taking place. On the other
hand, Mrs Hill tells me that she had lunch with a
number of friends and in the circumstances I can't
imagine anyone not telling the whole story.' Mrs Hill
nodded. 'It would have been all over the place in an
hour or two.'

WPC Cotton turned her clear brown eyes on Mrs
Hill. 'Did you mention it to anyone other than your
lunch party?'

Mrs Hill looked guilty. 'Well, yes. There was my
insurance agent, who used to be a friend of my husband's. And my bank manager. And, of course, my
business had to be told where to find me. There may
have been somebody else. I just don't remember. My
head was buzzing.'

'And your cousin in Edinburgh?' I asked.

'I tried but he wasn't answering his phone.' Mrs
Hill looked harassed beyond belief. 'Somebody will tell
him. We know a lot of the same people. He has to
know some time, because he's my heir.'

WPC Cotton was looking less crisp and confident
and I decided that there was more than one reason

why she had been saddled with this interview. But she had the gift of persistence. 'You told all of them of the plan to bury your dog in the lawn here?'

'I expect I did. It all seemed to be part and parcel. Besides, it was so strange! It was enough to keep conversation flowing instead of turning into awkward silences.'

'But you didn't mention the autopsy and the visit of the technician to any of them?'

'Not that I remember,' Mrs Hill said airily.

'Please write me out a list of everybody you told. Names and addresses or phone numbers. Give it to the officer who comes to take casts of those footprints. And add to it or let me know if you remember anyone else.'

Mrs Hill promised faithfully to do so.

WPC Cotton closed her shorthand book and seemed about to leave, but before moving she looked into our faces and said, 'Can any of you suggest any reason in the world why somebody might steal the corpse of the dog? Other than a fear, almost certainly mistaken, that there might be some evidence attaching to it that might identify him?'

Mrs Hill looked blank. I suppose that I did the same. The suggestion that I had voiced earlier now seemed too whimsical to repeat.

'Has anything been learned from the fibres between the dog's teeth?' I asked.

'I don't know,' the WPC said flatly. She did not have to add that even if she had known the answer she would have kept it to herself.

Beth cleared her throat shyly. 'Mrs Kitts told us

that she'd preserved Atilla's stomach contents for the police but the . . . the culprit might not realize that. He might have been after something small but valuable but Atilla chased him until he dropped it and Atilla then swallowed it. So you may find the answer in what Isobel sent to the lab.'

The WPC looked doubtful but thanked her for the suggestion. 'Do you – or did you – have anything "small but valuable"?' she asked Mrs Hill.

'Yes, of course I did,' Mrs Hill said. She seemed surprised that anybody might lack small valuables. 'Jewellery and so on, mostly. If they find a ring or something in Atilla's stomach, I suppose I'll get it back?'

To the dogs, and therefore necessarily to us, one day of the week was much the same as another. We tended to lose track of the days and I had quite forgotten that it was Friday until Henry, Isobel's husband, walked in.

Henry had enjoyed a successful career in banking. He is substantially older than Isobel – who sometimes jokingly insists that she was a child bride – but he had recently undergone a remarkable rejuvenation. True, he was still as bald as the proverbial egg except for a wispy fringe of white, his face was still folded into creases resembling those of an elderly bloodhound and he always hobbled stiffly for the first hundred yards or so until his joints worked themselves loose. But the idleness of retirement had never suited him. Sometimes I had thought that he was doing no more than dawdling along, waiting for death. But all that had changed when he, along with a solicitor, had become the executors of the estate of an extremely wealthy old friend and trustee to the wayward granddaughter. These new responsibilities and a consequent return into that world of business which he had quitted reluctantly and sorely missed had put a fresh gleam in his eye and even a trace of a spring in his step. Unfortunately the new lifestyle had also put an inch or two onto his waistline, as Isobel never hesitated to point out, but she admitted that that was a small price to pay for a husband who was not only contented and fully occupied but spent much of his time happily in the Borders instead of moping around at home.

Henry and Isobel stayed to eat with us, as they often did, especially when Henry was at home. Eight of us around the big kitchen table was a crush, but it made a sociable crowd and we lingered at table while a bottle of wine went round. Henry, whose circle of acquaintances is wide, turned out to have known Mr and Mrs Hill and to have had them for friends as well as clients at some time in the past, and he treated her with a courtly deference which she seemed to find much to her taste. Daffy left for home while Hannah and Sam went for a last look at the dogs. We were free to discuss the events of the previous few days and to tell Henry about it in more detail than Isobel had conveyed over the phone.

Mrs Hill had shaken off her nerves and tearfulness and was delighting in being the centre of attention. But Henry, innocently I believe, put an end to that. 'Somebody doesn't like you very much,' he told her.

view of the absence c
a burglar would fit tl
did no more than mal
just now. My mind m

Henry's mind m
morning, but mine w

There was a murmur of agreement. Nobody of our acquaintance liked Mrs Hill very much.

The police had not finished with us for that day. Mrs Hill was in full flood, regaling us again with the story of her shock at finding her home ablaze and her distress at Atilla's fate (to which she had now added her puzzlement as to who might have removed the corpse of Atilla and why anyone could possibly hold her in such dislike) when we saw lights and heard a vehicle arrive.

Mrs Hill, relying on her status as a visitor, would not have disturbed herself to go to the door. Beth was sewing, Isobel was out of the room and Henry was obviously tired, so I got out of my chair on weary legs and reached the front door just as the bell sounded.

On the doorstep I found DI Burrard, accompanied by a hawk-faced individual. They had come, Burrard said, to interview Mrs Hill. Again.

I took them into the sitting room, added a couple of logs to the still smouldering fire and went to invite our visitor to join them. She frowned, but in irritation rather than fear. 'I've already told them everything I know,' she grumbled.

'I'm afraid you're going to have to tell them again,' I told her. 'As a case develops, they keep coming across areas they need to know more about. They may even have a special reason, like making a case against some individual.'

'I suppose so.' She turned to Henry. 'Mr Kitts . . . Henry . . . would you come and be with me?'

I was consciou
My dislike of Mrs
loss, was becomir
but illogically I fel
her dependence tc

'Dear lady,' He
derous, Victorian
concerned, perhaj
with you.'

She shook her
reason to be afraic
with me for moral

Henry seemed
than I did. The two
room. Isobel, when
She kept looking at
no business impos
time that we got ои

After an age t
police vehicle drov
the kitchen.

'Mrs Hill's gone
you'll see her agaiı
expect, has been ide
It's been confirme
deliberately. And t
information. Despit
been found of the c

'They asked a
relationship betwe
doubt that they thir
for both the death

Chapter Four

I was jerked awake at about two in the morning when Mrs Hill's Audi exploded. It is not always easy to recall the moment of waking, especially when you thought, as I did, that it was all part of a horrible dream, but Beth and I later managed to piece it together. First, the dogs in the kennels began to bark. The police were convinced that there must have been the sound of a shot or a blow as the fuel tank was holed, but we are both fairly sure that there was no such noise, just a sudden roar as free petrol was ignited followed ten seconds later by an escalation of the noise as the tank was ruptured too completely for anyone ever to be sure whether it had been holed or not. Even through the curtains, the room was filled with flickering light and the smell of burning.

How Sam managed to sleep through it all I shall never know. We can only be thankful. Truly the sleep of a child is a deep sleep. There was instant pandemonium. Beth was shrieking at me to put some clothes on though I was already struggling into my trousers and I was never in any danger of being cold. I shouted at her to phone the emergency services. Mrs Hill was in the hall in a frivolous nightdress more suitable for a teenager, demanding that somebody do something to save her car although it was already far too late for that. The dogs in their kennels were kicking up an almighty row. And above it all was the infernal roar of the flames.

Luckily, Mrs Hill had parked her Audi some yards from our wall or the house might have caught; my car, which had fetched supplies from Cupar during the afternoon, was at the back of the house and Hannah's Lotus was with her at Daffy's cottage. The gravel sloped away from the house, so the liquid fire had spread along the drive. That far and no further luck was with us. As it was, I burst out of the front door carrying our two extinguishers, to be met by a staggering blast of heat and the smells of burning. I used up one extinguisher on the car, with very little effect. I used the second extinguisher on the front door and along the eaves. The glass in the windows was already cracking.

I ducked back indoors. I had achieved little enough but I could do nothing more except wait to see whether the fire burned itself out before the fire brigade arrived. I gathered two buckets of water and stood by in case the windows fell out, but we were spared total disaster. Beth, meantime, kept her head, made sure that the back door was unbolted and then went to sit with the still sleeping Sam, ready to evacuate in a hurry if the house caught fire. Mrs Hill, we discovered later, had for once kept her head and had been frantically packing her new wardrobe, ready to take it all with her if necessary. In about ten minutes, when the flames were beginning to die down of their own accord, the first fire appliance arrived from Cupar and soon brought the remains of the blaze under control.

Our outside light had died the death. In the returning darkness and deep chill, by the lights of the fire-fighting vehicle, I took stock, along with a dozen or so bystanders attracted from the village by the excitement. Mrs Hill's Audi under a blanket of foam was barely recognizable as having once been a car. In comparative darkness, and with my mind still stunned from being whisked out of deep sleep, I could only review the damage without quite taking it in. The front door was charred, the stone was blackened and the windows would have to be replaced. Some of the grass and one flowerbed were ruined and the slime of foam was over much of the gravel. The older of my two sheepskin coats was only fit for the dustbin, where Beth had long been wanting to dispose of it. I seemed to have lost some hair.

Hannah and Daffy had been woken by the klaxons and had rushed from the village. Like most of the bystanders, they were in furry boots and warm coats over nightwear. They reported that now that the furore was over the dogs were settling down to sleep again. I sent the two back to their beds. Somebody would have to be up and about in the morning and I had a feeling that that person would not be me.

As I feared, the emergency services were less easily dismissed. I gave them my attention while Beth coped with the distraught Mrs Hill. The firemen were not going to leave without making sure that nothing was smouldering and their leader, along with the local

constable, wanted to know how the fire had started –
a question which I was quite unable to answer.

The sun rises late over Scotland near midwinter,
but there were signs of grey dawn over the North Sea
before we got to our beds. The only emotion I was
capable of feeling was thankfulness. It could have been
so very much worse.

Before I was properly asleep again I was half-roused
by noises as Hannah set to work and Daffy, the only
one to remember our commitments, went off in my
car to collect Isobel, who was due to run Aspen in a
novice stake somewhere in Angus. They could guess,
bless them, that we would be desperate to make up
for lost sleep. Beth and I were each determined to get
up and see to Sam, letting the other lie in; but we both
went into deep sleep and it was left to Henry, walking
over to see what he could do to help, to get Sam up
and give him a breakfast of sorts. Sam was first puzzled
by the mess and then furious at having missed all the
fun.

When I awoke, half-slept but only too aware of
much to be done, the sun was well up in the sky. Beth
was finishing getting dressed. I followed her downstairs as soon as I was respectable and I hurried outside
to see if the house was in as much of a mess as I
thought. And it was. I was awake now and the damage
was exposed to the pitiless light of day. Nothing had
gone away or healed up in the night. An hour of rain
just after dawn had washed away or compacted some
of the foam, but only to reveal the gravel below,

blackened by soot and churned up by heavy vehicles. My mood of thankfulness and the complacency of years were long gone. The solid old farmhouse, friendly of aspect and always looking as loved as pristine paintwork could make it, now had the air of an elderly vagrant found drunk and dying in a ditch. The familiar shape was there but it was cloaked in foulness. Our safe refuge was not safe any more.

I pulled myself together. A lot of work would be needed but it could be accomplished. Given time, even the Virginia creeper would regenerate. The sooner work began, the better. I took the phone to the breakfast table with me, pausing in mid-cereal to phone my insurance agent in Dundee. While eating the boiled egg that was as much as I could fancy by way of a cooked breakfast, I summoned the builder who had done most of the work on the house and kennels and between slices of toast I called the garage and asked them to remove the remains of Mrs Hill's car.

Henry joined us in the kitchen for coffee and talk and the sound of his voice eventually brought Mrs Hill out of hiding. She wore a very smart dress – she did not have any other kind – but without make-up and with her hair only hastily dressed she looked both exhausted and many years older than what I believed to be her true age, give or take a decade or so.

Henry had already heard from Daffy that Mrs Hill's car had burned in the night – which he could now see for himself – and that we had no idea how or why. Henry was getting on in years and his memory for names was already fading, but his mind was as sharp as ever and he could think a subject through quicker than anyone I knew.

'Two things jump to mind,' he said. He looked at Mrs Hill. 'Assuming that this is no mere series of coincidences, either somebody has a grudge against you—'

'Well, I can't think who,' she said.

Henry looked at her for a second but refrained from comment. 'Perhaps not. But that doesn't mean that there isn't such a person. It may even be that the grudge is imaginary. He's now destroyed almost everything you owned. All that remains is your money and your person. We shall have to guard you well.' (Mrs Hill managed to look both frightened and gratified. I could see the prospect of getting rid of her receding into the dim distance.) 'The alternative,' Henry resumed, 'is that somebody may feel a need to destroy something which he thinks, rightly or wrongly, is in your possession.'

'Well, really!' Mrs Hill snorted.

'Yes, really. It could be something you're unaware of, even something you never set eyes on, but if somebody thought that you had it, that would explain a succession of fires, perhaps more believably than the idea of a vendetta against yourself. In which case . . .'

'In which case,' I finished for him, 'whoever it is may think that whatever it is is now in this house. Excuse me.'

I got up and went to take the cordless phone off its base on the wall. I wanted my two fire extinguishers refilled immediately and another four supplied on sale or return. To the same order I added, as an afterthought, four smoke alarms to add to the two already installed. As I made my call I could hear Mrs Hill protesting that nobody could possibly believe that she had ever had anything in the house which was in the least *threatening* or *incriminating* to anybody. She managed to express this viewpoint many times without repeating herself.

'Believe that if you want to,' Henry said. 'John will be well advised to take precautions. And when the police return—'

'They won't, will they?'

'Without a doubt. And when they do, you may care to remember that, from the viewpoint of the police, the only alternative to the two possibilities I've just suggested may be that you yourself . . . Well, you could see the direction their minds were taking.'

That at least silenced Mrs Hill for the moment.

I had doubts as to whether this was going to be my day for getting through a lot of training, but I had to try. I got as far as the barn with a brace of very young trainees when the insurance agent arrived. (This remarkably prompt service stemmed from the fact that he owed me a favour for retraining a German short-haired pointer which had developed the regrettable habit of peeing on its retrieves.) He had already spoken to the Fire Investigator but had decided that, whatever the cause of the fire and whether or not the company might have later recourse against a culprit, the burning of somebody else's car on my doorstep was a risk covered by my policy. We agreed the scope of the work and he left me a claim form to fill out as soon as I had an estimate.

Back to the barn, minutes before the builder turned up. He promised to replace the cracked panes immediately, took note of the soot-stained stonework, the blistered timber and the churned and blackened drive, measured the windows and thought that he could telephone me an estimate within two days.

I had taken a few paces in the direction of the barn when the next arrivals dead-heated. The recovery vehicle from the garage gave way to the police Range Rover at our gates and followed it up the driveway. I waved the driver of the tow truck forward to halt beside the burned-out wreck.

DI Burrard erupted out of the Range Rover. 'What's going on?' he demanded.

'I'm having this wreck hauled away,' I told him.

'No, you're not. This wreck is evidence.'

I am usually a pussycat to deal with – or so I keep assuring Beth – but while I was in the army I had had more than enough of being arbitrarily ordered about. Attempts to push me around without good reason always bring out the worst in me. Furthermore, I was well into my mood for riding roughshod over obstacles. 'Then have it outside your own front door,' I told him. 'It doesn't stay outside mine. Are you going to collect it? Or shall I have it sent?'

He only hesitated for a second, wondering how far he could stretch his powers. 'I'll have it collected.'

'Right.' I turned to the driver. 'Come back in an hour. If it's still here, take it away and, as far as I'm concerned, lose it.'

The driver, who was in the habit of beating on one of the local shoots, knew me well. He grinned. 'I'll do that,' he said.

The hawk-faced man had followed the DI out of the Range Rover. Burrard turned on him. 'Sergeant Forsyth, get on to HQ. I want this wreckage collected at once.'

'Sir.'

The driver grinned even more widely. 'The usual way of it, they'll call me to lift it to Cupar for them.'

The DI took several deep breaths. I could see him thinking that the stars in their courses were fighting against him, or however policemen express such sentiments. 'Very well,' he said grittily. 'You do that. I'll clear the paperwork later.'

'But before it goes,' I said, 'there's something I want to look at.' I approached the wreck. The smell of burned paint and plastic was still almost overpowering. The Sergeant was speaking on the radio but Burrard was close at hand and looking over my shoulder. I had no objection. 'Take a look,' I told him. 'The trapdoor over the fuel filler seems to have been forced.'

'For all you can tell,' he said, 'it could have been bent when the fuel tank burst.'

That was true. The metal was twisted and the surface scorched. 'The filler cap's missing,' I pointed out.

'Blown off at the same time.'

'In which case,' I said, 'it would be over by the house wall, which it isn't.' With the tyres burned away the remains of the car were sitting very low and even in my working trousers I was not going to kneel down on the still warm, sooty gravel but I managed to crouch enough for a one-eyed glimpse under the remains of the car. 'It may be underneath,' I said. 'I can see something that may or may not be it. It could hardly have blown there.' I caught the driver's eye and he nodded.

'It might have bounced off something,' Burrard said doubtfully.

'But off what? It seems more likely to me that somebody forced the lid, took off the filler cap and dropped it or threw it away and then used a piece of hose to siphon petrol onto the ground. Then he tossed a match from a safe distance and ran for it.'

'I'm going to have the wreck examined,' Burrard said firmly. 'Then I'll draw my own conclusions. Meantime, I want to speak further with Mrs Hill.'

'Wait here,' I told him. Before he could object I slipped inside and closed the door.

Beth and Hannah, accompanied by Sam, had disappeared about the firm's business, but Henry and Mrs Hill had transferred to the sitting room and were filling out claim forms in front of a bright and cheerful fire. If this went on I would have to order more logs. I repeated the Detective Inspector's demand for an interview.

Mrs Hill, who had begun to relax, became flustered again. 'Oh dear!' she said. 'Again? Do I have to?'

Henry looked into the flames while he pondered. 'Strictly speaking,' he said, 'I think not. If you refuse to say anything to them, they could arrest you, in which case they have to charge you with something within six hours or let you go again. If you've done anything that you shouldn't, it's high time that you had a solicitor. But if you're quite innocent they can't possibly have enough evidence to justify arresting a respectable lady.'

'I should think not, indeed.' Mrs Hill sounded indignant that anyone should dare even to mention such a possibility. 'I have done nothing to be ashamed of and I have no idea what's behind it all.'

'So if you refuse, they'll just have to manage without you. On the other hand, that wouldn't be helping them to explain the death of your housekeeper or the fire at your house, the burning of your car or the theft of Atilla's body, and your various insurers might be displeased if it came to their attention, as such things all too often do. It would not look good. You really should see them.'

'Will you stay with me?'

'If that's what you want,' Henry said patiently.

I went to the door and told the Detective Inspector that Mrs Hill and Mr Kitts would see them together.

The clouds had blown away and we were again being presented with one of those unexpectedly fine winter days which can appear, like a flower among weeds, to chase away the blues. I began an intensive round of training on the grass that passes for lawn, keeping my back turned firmly to the oblique view of the fire's aftermath. This was intended to rescue my mind from dwelling on arson and sudden death and it succeeded. I was immersed in the lesser problems of inattention, incomprehension and plain disobedience when Henry came to find me. I looked around and suffered a renewed sense of shock at the ruined scene. Several patient individuals, whom I took to be Scene of Crime Officers, were now scraping the scorched gravel into bags, which I supposed would save the builder the trouble. The burned-out Audi had already vanished. Lunch, Henry said, would be on the table in ten minutes or so.

I had a quick word with the searchers. They were typically reticent but admitted that no filler cap had been found under the burnt car.

Henry came with me as I took the last brace of young dogs back to their kennels. He was anxious – and letting it show in small, nervous gestures, which for him was exceptional. 'It doesn't look too good,' he said. 'The body's been identified positively as being Elsie Bland. But I think you knew that already. A shame. I met her once. She was a pleasant young woman.

'I pressed for more information, on the grounds that I would advise Mrs Hill not to answer questions if she was kept completely in the dark as to their significance. Burrard tried veiled threats but eventually gave in. According to the police, there was a skull fracture but the pathologist still can't be sure that it hadn't been caused by half the house coming down on top of her. The body was badly burned but he was surprised at how little soot was found in what was left of the lungs, so it seems probable that she died before the fire. And although the fire seems to have started in the vicinity of the central-heating boiler, the police are sure that petrol was used to get it going. Why would that be? I thought domestic heating oil would do the job.'

'Given time to soak into wood, or anything else porous,' I explained, 'it can burn like petrol. But with a puddle of it lying on top of – what?'

'Floor tiles,' Henry said.

'On top of floor tiles, much might depend on temperature but I think you'd be likely to get a lot more smoke than heat.'

'Ah. So it seems probable that Miss Bland was knocked on the head and the fire was then started to cover up the evidence of the first crime.'

I kennelled the two dogs, giving each a pat, a word of praise and a biscuit from the hoard in my pocket. 'What else have they found out?' I asked as we started back towards the house.

'Quite a lot. Of course, they weren't here to keep us informed, but my bluff did extract a certain amount of information and more was spilled in the process of asking Mrs Hill to explain it. The major item was that Elsie Bland did not have a sister, in Balcraigs or anywhere else. She was an only child. They've checked at Register House.'

I slowed my pace. This was becoming almost interesting. 'So where did she go on her afternoons?' I asked.

'That is exactly what the police wanted to know.'

'And Mrs Hill couldn't enlighten them?'

'Of course not. She had already told them the story as she had received it from Miss Bland and she stuck to it.

'Then they dropped another bombshell. It seems

that Miss Bland had a bank account in Cupar holding a substantial sum and showing dividends from investments. They gave no details, but clearly Miss Bland need not have worked. Again. Mrs Hill stated flatly that she knew nothing about it. And I believed her on both counts.'

'More to the point, did the police believe her?'

'I think it's too early for belief or disbelief. But you could tell a lot from the slant of their questions. They wanted to know whether Miss Bland could have had a secret lover or any other kind of a secret life and, in the teeth of the evidence, Mrs Hill insisted that she could hardly credit such a thing. Then, until she was beginning to foam at the mouth and I had to call a halt, they probed into the relationship between the two women. They didn't miss a trick. They suggested the possibility of blackmail or some sort of conspiracy, or envy. They even hinted at a lesbian relationship until it was clear that Mrs Hill didn't understand what they were talking about. She was left in no doubt that they think she may have killed her housekeeper and set fire to the house. Or possibly the other way around, that Miss Bland came back unexpectedly and caught her setting the fire and got a knock on the head for her pains. It seems that Mrs Hill's insurance, while not excessive for a substantial house in prime condition, housing a collection of Wemyss ware, some other good antiques and the kind of wardrobe and jewellery to be expected of a film star, added up to the sort of sum which could be counted on to stagger a provincial Scottish cop. I pointed out that Mrs Hill was the principal shareholder in a substantial business and they dropped hints that the business might have required extra capital to prop it up. That, I think, was blind guesswork but it caused ripples – simply, I discovered, because, despite clinging to the Chair for no better reason than the status that it conveyed, Mrs Hill trusted her staff totally and was satisfied with having almost no real idea of what was going on.'

We had halted and lowered our voices as we came near the house. 'She needn't get too worried just yet,' I said. 'There are dozens of other possible explanations.'

'That's what I told her. But she's gone to lie down with an ice-bag on her forehead. She wants me to look into things for her. As it happens, I don't have to go back to Edinburgh this month, so I suppose I'll have to do it.'

'Oh, come on, Henry,' I protested. 'If she's worried, she should consult a solicitor, an accountant or a private detective. She has no right to push her burdens off onto you. Surely you don't have a fondness for her?'

Henry shrugged. 'Her late husband was a close personal friend of mine as well as being a client at the bank. I was very much attached to them as a couple and twenty years ago she was a very attractive woman. She was also rather a silly one, but silliness can seem a rather endearing characteristic in somebody else's wife, for short periods at a time. If that constitutes having a fondness, then perhaps I do have one. Anyway, I said that I'd try to help. So think over what we've said and we'll speak again. I could use some of those other possible explanations you mentioned.'

The weekend being upon us Sam was at home and at the lunch table, insisting on more than his fair share of food and attention. Mrs Hill was absent, so it was possible to avoid entirely the subject of her woes. Sam could hardly have failed to realize that something was amiss, with policemen sniffing around like spaniels on the trail of rabbits, but he had also discovered that that area of discussion was taboo. We ate our usual light meal in peace.

As soon as Beth was satisfied that I had swallowed at least the basic minimum necessary for survival, I made an excuse and Henry and I adjourned to the sitting room, still warm and firelit from the morning's occupation. We settled in the deep chairs, but not before I had poured us a dram of whisky apiece to lubricate the thinking processes.

Henry had provided himself with a notebook from the office. He took out his own very expensive pen. 'Now,' he said. 'Help me to analyse the possibilities logically. Let's start from the standpoint that Mrs Hill may be guilty of something. I think it's very unlikely, knowing the lady. She has neither the need nor the intelligence for crime. But it may help us to understand whatever line the police take.

'For a start, I discount absolutely the idea of a lesbian relationship between the two women.'

'Also because of knowing the lady?' I asked suggestively.

He gave me a look of reproach. 'Not the way you mean,' he said. 'My knowledge of her stops short of the carnal and is destined to stay that way. *Anno Domini* would ensure it even if my resolve should weaken. But after knowing both her and her late husband for some years I have no doubt of her sexual orientation. I could more easily believe that she has taken a male lover, even a toyboy. Not that she ever seemed highly sexed, but she's very much aware of men.'

'She seems to set store by appearances,' I said. 'How far would she go to protect a secret of that kind?'

That made Henry stop and think. 'Not very far,' he said at last. 'For one thing, she's a passive rather than an aggressive person. For another, she's always been openly flirtatious. It's tempting to think that she's past the age and condition in which she would attract a lover, but when you look around some of the liaisons which come to the surface you have to admit that no one is too old or too hideous. If it happened, I think that she'd be torn between preserving the secret and boasting about it.'

'Unless the lover was vulnerable? Or disreputable?'

'You're suggesting that Miss Bland threatened exposure? And Evelyn Hill knocked her on the head and then burned her own house to cover her tracks? I hate to admit it, but it's faintly possible. Rather drastic, but possible in theory. On the other hand, she sets great store by possessions. Saddled with a body, her mind, if she can be said to have one, would turn rather towards faking a burglary. We'll bear in mind the chance of any kind of a guilty secret.'

He wrote a few words in his beautiful italic script. 'We'll call those Possibilities One A to D,' he said. 'Moving on to Section Two, suppose she knew some-

64

body else's secret and she was the intended victim of a plot which went horribly wrong.'

'I don't see a middle-aged, respectable lady coming by anybody's guilty secret,' I objected.

'Don't you? I do. She has a host of friends of similar class, status and interests. Any one of them could be indiscreet and then regret it. Also, there's her late husband's firm.'

That took me by surprise. I had assumed that the lady was no more than a figurehead. 'You said that she was still in the chair, but you also said that she took little direct interest. Does she play an active enough part to uncover any malpractice?' I asked.

'Well, she is Chairman. Refuses to compromise and be called "chairperson", and quite right too. She doesn't play a very active part these days, just goes over once a week to sign things and chairs a board meeting now and again, but she does seem to make a half-hearted effort to keep abreast of what goes on. Of course, that can be a far cry from *understanding* what passes under her nose. Frankly, I'd be surprised if there wasn't a modicum of hanky-panky thereabouts.'

'You would? Why's that?'

'The situation invites it. I suppose I'll have to visit the factory with her.' Henry yawned as post-prandial torpor began to creep over him.

'None of your theories so far explains the burning of the Audi,' I pointed out.

'Not yet. But a connection could emerge, if somebody suspected that a clue to the secret was contained in the car. Letters, perhaps, of which she hadn't yet seen the significance.'

'Nor have you explained the grave-robbery.'

'Ah. There you have me. If there's an explanation that embraces all the known facts, other than coincidence or somebody who hates Mrs Hill so intensely that they wish to strip her of every last souvenir of her previous existence, I haven't thought of it so far. Let's file that in the *Too Difficult* basket and move on. Section Three, somebody was after Miss Bland. This, after all, is what happened; but we've no indication at the moment that she was anything other than an unfortunate lady who was in the wrong place at the wrong time. Four, burglary or similar. They wanted something in the house and Miss Bland, who was supposed to be out, disturbed them and paid the price.' He yawned again. 'What have I missed?'

'Not a lot,' I said.

'You're wrong. Miss Bland was a wealthy woman. Five. I'd better find out who expects to inherit. And . . . and . . .'

Henry was in the habit of taking a nap after lunch. He put his head back and was asleep immediately. I tiptoed out of the room.

I decided on a quick half-hour with Jasper. Jasper was that perennial thorn in the trainer's flesh, a spaniel of wholly show-bench breeding. Jasper's owner, a keen shooting man, was well aware that such breeding, which concentrates on beauty and strict conformation to an arbitrary Kennel Club breed standard with only token consideration given to stamina and even less to intelligence, can produce dogs of considerable beauty which lack the nous to recognize their own names. Some of them are barely able to scratch without falling over. Jasper (like the late Atilla) had been one of these. The end product of an unplanned mating, he had been a present to the owner from the owner's god-daughter, so he told me, and Jasper was therefore a fixture. He had been brought to me to see what I could make of him or, in the last resort, to have an unfortunate accident that involved Jasper and a load of shot. It was not an uncommon story. As long as his owner was prepared to pay me for keeping Jasper I was prepared to persevere, but sometimes I felt that Jasper's life hung by a thread and I was saddened, because he was an attractive and affectionate animal.

My half-hour stretched to nearly an hour because we seemed to be making progress at last. I had previously found it possible to teach him the elements, such as his own name, to come to the whistle, to sit and to walk at heel with only occasional lapses; but those lessons were invariably forgotten by next day. This time, however, they seemed to have been retained and after brief refresher exercises we moved on. Late in the lesson, he was carrying a dummy reliably at heel so I decided to shoot for the moon and try him on a retrieve. I threw the dummy across the lawn, kept him sitting for a count of ten and then let him go for it. I watched in my peripheral vision as, to my delight, he retrieved it, if not exactly to hand at least to drop it beside my foot, looking up at me with as much pride as if he had just explained relativity.

I made an appropriate fuss of him and decided to consolidate the lesson but, at the next try, the result was less propitious. I threw the dummy with more vigour than I had intended and at first bounce it reached the edge of the shrubbery which borders the high garden wall along the road. Rashly, I sent Jasper anyway. He sniffed along the edge of the shrubbery, moving away from where the dummy had fallen, ignored my signals, gave me one puzzled but forgiving look and picked up something smaller and round. When he reached me and – *mirabile dictu!* – delivered it to hand, sitting, I found that it was an indubitable filler cap, clean and not even sooty. Jasper was looking at me anxiously. With my fingers crossed, I assured him that he had done brilliantly. He seemed pleased. He meant well, I decided. Given double the brain cells he might become a passable performer.

I returned him to his kennel and went back to the house.

Chapter Five

Henry was awake. I met him in the hall, heading in search of refreshing tea for his dry mouth. Tea seemed like a good idea to me too. I led him into the kitchen and put the still warm kettle on again. Beth had gone out, probably to help with the daily feed.

Henry settled in one of the basket chairs and I held out the filler cap. 'What's this?' he said. His mind was still dull from sleep.

'I think it's the Audi's filler cap. Jasper found it in the shrubs at the far side of the lawn.' I put aside the temptation to swerve onto the subject of Jasper's progress. 'It was nearer to the gate than to the car, which explains why the police didn't find it. I think that somebody forced the cover, took off the filler cap, siphoned petrol out onto the ground and dropped a match. Then, as he was making for the gate, he realized that he still had the cap and he threw it away.'

Henry's wits were returning. 'Why would Jasper bring this in preference to, say, a stick?'

It was a good point. 'Perhaps,' I said slowly, 'he detected the scent of somebody he knew.'

Henry accepted the object from me. 'Ugh! It's all slimy!'

'It spent half a minute in Jasper's mouth.'

Henry handed me back the cap and got up to wash his hands at the sink. 'Should we be handling it like this?' he asked.

'Probably not. But after being thoroughly licked by Jasper I wouldn't expect it to carry any fingerprints. Not that that stippled finish would take prints anyway. We'll have to show the police where it was found, which will finish any chance of suggesting that the Audi was a victim of spontaneous combustion.'

'That may be to the good,' Henry said thoughtfully. 'Mrs Hill would have no reason to burn her own car.'

'The police might argue that she was cashing in all her assets with the intention of fleeing the country ahead of some disaster still to be revealed. It could even be true. You're still determined to help her?'

'Not determined, no. I wouldn't put it as strongly as that. Let's just say that I feel obliged. I owe that much to her husband. He was good company and he gave me some valuable tips.'

'On the stock market?'

'Horses.'

I paused to choose my words carefully. 'I'll do what I can to help,' I said. 'But Rex will be back from offshore, probably on Tuesday, and they won't have room for Hannah. And Mrs Hill is occupying Hannah's room. You, on the other hand, have a permanent spare room and the lady is a friend of yours. We hardly know her.'

There was no need to go on. I could see that Henry was fighting to conceal his horror at the suggestion. But he was still a quick thinker. 'Yes, of course,' he said. 'We could easily give Hannah a bed. It would be better not to move Mrs Hill again, just when she seems to be settling down.' He changed the subject quickly before I could produce further arguments. 'I want to go and have a look at what's left of the house. Come with me?'

I thought about it and decided that I would be interested. 'But,' I said, 'the light would be almost gone before we could get there. Tomorrow morning?'

'Fine. And, John, I'd be easier in my mind if we had some indication as to the sort of questions the police are asking. We should try to speak to one or two locals. Do you have any contacts at Kirktillem?'

On the point of shaking my head, I remembered. 'I've met a farmer,' I said. 'His name was McRodgers. I think his farm is adjacent to Atherton House. In fact, I think the farm's name is Atherton.'

'Well, it's a start,' Henry said doubtfully.

Almost immediately, I was able to confirm the farmer's name and his farm's juxtaposition to Mrs Hill's former place of abode. The lady herself made another appearance and eagerly accepted tea and biscuits. She had made an effort to smarten herself up. Her hair was once again immaculate but under the careful make-up I could detect the lines of stress and the pallor of sleeplessness.

Mr McRodgers, she said, was a very mean-spirited man who would probably refuse to help if he could possibly avoid it and any help he did offer should not be taken at face value, but she couldn't imagine what we thought he'd be able to tell us because he never seemed to think about anything but his crops. He could, I thought, probably tell us who else might be able to say something useful, but there was no point embarking on a lengthy explanation. 'What can you tell us about Miss Bland?' I asked her.

Mrs Hill put first things first. If there had been any kind of friction between the two women, she was a remarkably good actress. 'Elsie was a very good cook and housekeeper,' she said, 'and not one of those who are always asking for more and more wages. And she was a nice person. Sometimes she seemed more like a friend than an employee.'

'Did she ever seem to have more money than you expected?'

'The police asked me that. So did Henry. I can only repeat myself. She sometimes bought herself a little present, like her motor scooter, but she explained to me that her parents had left her a little money and that she'd been well advised when she invested it. She said that it might have been just enough to live on but there would have been no margin for a social life. She preferred to earn her keep and have something in hand to play with.'

I still had no mental picture of the late Miss Bland. 'I suppose any photographs of her were lost in the fire?' I suggested.

On the point of nodding her head, Mrs Hill suddenly stopped and laughed. 'Aren't I the silly one?' she demanded of anyone within earshot. Without ill-advisedly waiting for an answer, she said, 'I left some film for developing and printing in Cupar just the other day when I went in with my cleaning and with all the kerfuffle I forgot all about them. Three whole cassettes going back to the early summer. Henry, may I borrow your car? The chemist will still be open.'

Henry did not seem taken with the idea and I could not blame him. Cars driven by Mrs Hill might prove to have a limited life. 'I'll drive you into Cupar,' he said. 'And, while we're there, perhaps you should consider buying or hiring another car. After all, you were adequately insured.'

Mrs Hill forgot her woes and her eyes lit up, presumably at the prospect of going on another shopping spree with money which the insurance company would eventually refund. 'Wait while I fetch my coat,' she said.

'You have the receipt for your films?'

'It was in the handbag that I've had with me all along.'

While she was out of the room, I looked at Henry and found that he was looking at me. I said, 'Henry, are you thinking what I'm thinking?'

'If you're thinking,' Henry said, 'that this whole disaster may have been about the photographs, then I am. To take one possibility among many, suppose that during one of her jaunts abroad she caught, in the background of a holiday snap, a couple who should definitely not have been on holiday together. Either somebody well known or somebody known to someone in her own circle so that the photograph was certain to come to the wrong person's notice sooner or later. Mrs Hill might very well not have the faintest idea what dynamite she was carrying around in the form of a latent image.'

'It would explain everything except the theft of the

dog,' I said. 'So be careful. He or she may be confident that the photographs have been destroyed by now, but it might be a sensible move to leave the negatives for at least two more sets of prints.'

Henry nodded. 'I already had it at the forefront of my mind. You know, this could explain everything except the grave-robbery. Dare I suggest that the corpse of Atilla was dug up by a pack of hungry foxes?'

'No,' I said, 'you may not. Foxes are very solitary animals except during the breeding season, which this definitely is not. And we put Atilla well down with some heavy stones on top. Even a vixen with a couple of well-grown cubs still following her could have found easier prey. There are rabbits in the gorse and partridges roost on the ground. They'd be easier meat.'

'H'm,' said Henry. Mrs Hill came back just then, resplendent in a very fine Persian lamb coat, and they hurried off for fear of missing the chemist and having to wait until Monday.

With Isobel and Daffy away and Henry and me distracted, Beth, Hannah and Sam had had a busy day. I hurried to give some belated help and we finished up the inescapable chores as the last of the daylight died away. We washed all the dog-dishes and made preparations for our own evening meal in a last burst of energy and then retired to the sitting room where habit demanded a round of drinks and a comparing of notes.

I could sense that Beth was bursting with questions, but with Sam present, sitting quietly with his glass of Coke but absorbing every word, they had to wait. It was Sam himself who almost opened up the subject. 'Dad,' he said, 'is that woman going to stay here for always?'

'No, she is definitely not,' Beth said firmly. She hurried across the hall to turn down the heat under the potatoes, but when she came back and resumed her seat she picked up the subject as though it had never been dropped. 'And don't you speak of her as "that woman",' she added severely. 'It's very rude. You're not to repeat a word of this, understood?'

Sam nodded seriously. (We had brought him to the point at which he had learned to respect confidentiality, provided that we remembered to get his undertaking. Otherwise, whatever was said in his presence soon became public property.)

Reassured, I mentioned my words with Henry and his evasion of my hint that Mrs Hill might be rehomed in his spare bedroom. 'I can try again,' I said.

'No, don't do that,' said Beth. 'That would seem like nagging. But, bearing in mind that I don't know a thing about what was said between you, I can try it on with Isobel.'

'Try very hard,' Hannah said. 'I want my room back. Daffy means well, but it isn't the same since she became a married woman.'

This I could understand. Daffy had a determined set to her jaw. The two kennelmaids were very alike in some ways and vastly different in others. They remained with us, I think, out of love and loyalty, not for us but for the dogs. 'She condescends to you as the spinster on the shelf?' I suggested.

Hannah smiled wryly. 'She does, rather.'

'If she did but know,' Beth said. Hannah, whose

love life could not entirely be hidden from us, blushed furiously.

It was a rule of the house that anyone absent when the evening meal was pronounced ready could expect no more than to find their portion saved in a warm oven. If it was dried to a consistency suitable for re-soling boots, the late comers could make use of the microwave to create something fresh. We never waited for absentees. Apart from the presence of a child in the house, delayed returns were too common and too unpredictable, food too tasty and hunger often too pressing.

The four of us sat down together at a table set for eight (because Isobel and Henry and Daffy often dined with us and always on the evening after a field trial). Minutes later Daffy and Isobel returned, with only a second place to show for all the effort and expense. Years before, this would have been cause for celebration; but as time went by we had become blasé about awards which did nothing to advance the dog towards the Field Trial Champion status which would figure in the pedigrees of our stock for another five gener-ations, but not so blasé as to show no interest. They were in the middle of an account of the trial, flush by flush and retrieve by retrieve, when Henry came back alone, thirsting for the drink that his errand of mercy had caused him to miss. Mrs Hill, he said, had retrieved her photographs, left the negatives for further printing and intended to have a trial drive of a new Mercedes. The garage proprietor had promised to see that she reached us safely. The car, if she confirmed the purchase, would be delivered to her on the Monday morning, freshly taxed.

Mrs Hill herself, elated by the fresh orgy of expenditure, arrived at last but she refused to part with her photographs until she had sifted through them herself. She had her little secrets, she said coyly. Daffy left for home and Hannah took Sam off to watch television, but the rest of us waited with the absolute minimum of polite patience while Mrs Hill ate her still warm and moist share of the casserole, maintaining meanwhile a commentary on the pros and cons affecting her latest prospective purchase. I could have forgiven a recitation about acceleration, smooth ride or handling qualities, but a disquisition on such matters as carpet colours and the smell of new leather only emphasized her unworthiness to own such machinery. But I contained myself and continued to do so while she fanned through more than a hundred enlargements and pronounced them innocuous. 'Or at least,' she said, 'if there's anything significant on any of them, I can't see it.'

At last we were allowed to see for ourselves. The table had been cleared and the photographs were now arranged in groups. The largest group, nearly half the total, had been taken during a cruise of the eastern Mediterranean and the Black Sea that Mrs Hill had taken in the late spring aboard a very upmarket Cunarder. She was able to identify everyone in the various foregrounds and also those who had been captured in her company in photographs taken with her camera by others. In most instances she was able to quote at least their area of residence and the husband's occupation and to favour us with as much of a potted biography as she had been able to glean, with footnotes on their personal habits and peculiarities. We jotted down the salient information on the backs of the prints. They seemed to furnish very poor material for blackmail, but in the backgrounds were many fellow-passengers, singles, couples and in groups. None of these, as far as any of us could recognize, had well-known faces nor looked unduly alarmed at being included in the photograph; but it would have been perfectly possible for an illicit couple to have been included, one or both of whom would have been instantly recognizable to somebody among Mrs Hill's friends.

A smaller group of photographs were a record of Mrs Hill's more valuable possessions, including her collection of Wemyss pottery. This record, she said immediately, would come in handy during the inevitable argument with her insurers. It was obvious from the photographs that the house would have been a prime target for knowledgeable robbers. Otherwise, those shots seemed to have little significance.

The remainder seemed mostly to have been taken as souvenirs of visitors at Atherton House. I had glimpsed the house from the road or the fields occasionally – a traditional Scottish house of stone and slate, very difficult to date but obviously quality built and commodious. I now saw that the house had seemed to be in very good condition and was set in a spacious garden that had been beautiful when the photographs were taken, in summer and before the arrival of the fire appliances.

Many of the shots in which Mrs Hill herself figured had been taken, she explained, by the late Elsie Bland; but Miss Bland, who had clearly been on very friendly terms with her employer, appeared in some of them. She was an unremarkable but not unattractive woman in what I judged to be her early thirties, with a round, friendly face that seemed to be either smiling or about to smile. I could envisage her as being everybody's friend or favourite aunt and yet there was character in the planes of her face and that character was by no means passionless. I had seen its like before among army wives and I thought that anyone daring to make a pass at Miss Bland might find that he had a tiger by the tail.

'Did she have rather unsightly wrists and ankles?' I asked suddenly.

Mrs Hill raised her eyebrows. 'Not that I ever noticed,' she said.

'You probably wouldn't. But I could be wrong. It's just that she has a good figure and yet she usually seems to have been wearing long sleeves even in hot weather and either trousers or unfashionable fashion boots. A woman with good wrists and ankles likes to show them off.'

In one of the photographs, Miss Bland was seated at a table in the garden of Atherton House, talking quietly with a man of about fifty-five. The man's face seemed familiar. It can sometimes be very difficult to identify a face seen suddenly and out of context. I had the man almost pegged as a Dundee taxi-driver and then as a teller in my bank before I realized that he was a client of the kennels. 'Isn't this Jasper's owner? Mr Hislop?'

'You know him?' Mrs Hill asked happily. 'That's my cousin, Irvine Hislop. He comes . . . came through now and again to Atherton House. In fact, after you did so well with poor Atilla and when Irvine was finding Jasper so difficult to train, I recommended him to you or you to him, whichever way it's supposed to be, but I forgot to ask him whether he'd taken my advice.'

I thanked her politely.

'I'm so glad that I was able to help both of you,' she said benignly.

We returned to studying the photographs. My magnifying glass was passed from hand to hand but without any useful discoveries being made.

'Leave them here for the moment,' I said. 'Then we'll be able to refer to them, if anyone suspicious arrives at the door.' Beth keeps a whole row of recipe-books on a shelf and I tucked the folders of photographs in among them.

Chapter Six

There was little to choose between the days of the week at Three Oaks. Dogs do not care what day it may be. They expect to be fed and cleaned and walked; and any break in the routine is taken for a sign that the world is coming to an end. Saturdays in autumn and winter, however, tend to be busy with competitions and therefore extra work for those who stay behind, and so on Sundays, unless it is my Masterclass day or Isobel decides to carry out a round of vaccinations or one of her regular purges against fleas, ticks, toxocara larvae and all the different species of worms that dogs are heir to, we allow ourselves a little latitude, starting later in the morning and giving the trainees a rest from their education.

Daffy, however, danced to a different rhythm. Instead of a weekly cycle, her labours were adjusted to her husband's shifts of two weeks offshore and then two weeks at home. With Rex's return almost due she was pulling more than her weight, laying up credit for the days ahead when he would expect first call on her attention.

The pleasure of lying abed on a cold morning, entwined with Beth, was doubled by the sound of

Daffy at work below. She was in her singing mood and, as so often, was amusing herself by mocking an old ballad. I listened. She had a pure, clear voice and I always enjoyed hearing Daffy in her old, rebellious vein.

Her voice and the clatter of the feeding trolley faded in the distance, to be replaced by the chatter of a skein of greylag geese far overhead, and I decided that it was time to get up.

Henry and Isobel arrived before I had quite finished helping with the chores. Mrs Hill was taking herself off to the kirk. I am not a churchgoer myself. I had recently seen a television programme about people who watched for space travellers, signalled to where their signals might be intercepted by them and virtually worshipped visitors, if any, from some other planet. Strange though their beliefs might be, I surprised myself by concluding that, by falling within the bounds of our natural philosophy, they were slightly more credible than the tenets of organized Christianity. Nevertheless, I usually try to avoid offending anyone else by too obviously abstaining from church or breaking the Sabbath. Henry and I sat down with a cup of coffee and went through the photographs again. They were no more informative than before, but we shared a feeling that familiarity with the images might pay off later.

After a decent interval, to allow the godly time to settle themselves in church, we set off in my car. Now that he had my attention and no other listeners, Henry said glumly, 'Mrs Hill comes to stay with us tomorrow.'

'Oh, yes?' I said carefully.

'Isobel invited her. She didn't want to but she can see what a drag Evelyn Hill is on the running of the kennels. You must have said something. And I may say that I thought better of you. You knew how I felt about her.'

'Much the same as I did,' I said. 'But I can assure you that I didn't say a word to Isobel.'

It was the literal truth but Henry grunted dubiously.

'Send her shopping for houses,' I told him. 'She'll enjoy it, it'll keep her out of your hair and she'll soon find something.'

'She'll probably decide to rebuild,' he said gloomily. 'And then we'll be stuck with her for months. And she'll still spend her days at Three Oaks.'

'Isobel will get sick of her within a couple of weeks,' I said. 'Then you can boot her out to the hotel, which is where she should have been all along, or send her off on a world cruise.'

Henry was not to be comforted. 'And suppose that whoever's behind it all decides to start a third fire? At least while she's at your house there's always some-body around, and you've got enough fire extinguishers to quench Cockenzie power station. Our house is empty most days.'

The risk seemed very remote. 'Treble your insurance,' I advised him. 'You might even show a profit.'

Henry uttered a caricature of a laugh, intended to demonstrate how unamused he was.

Twenty minutes brought us to the village of Kirk-tillem, no more than a street of small houses, a village shop, a Church of Scotland kirk and no less than three pubs, the whole set in level farmland. At the southern end of the village, about two acres of garden and trees embraced what remained of Atherton House. This had once been the residence of a minor landowner, but there had been a gambler in the family and eventually the estate had been broken up and the farms sold off.

Seen through the trees, I had held the impression that the house was of above average quality, an impression reinforced by glimpses in the background of Mrs Hill's photographs of stonework in rich-looking uncoursed, rock-faced, snecked ashlar (or so it was described to me by the man who came to clean the stonework at Three Oaks) complete with chiselled margins and crow-stepped gables – the very epitome of romantic Scottish vernacular at its most extravagant, a far cry from the sound, well-proportioned but utilitarian architecture of Three Oaks. As we came up the drive the shape of the house was revealed for the first time, and although the roof was now missing and sky showed through the upper window there was no doubt that it had been designed (rather than merely built) either in pursuit of beauty for its own sake or else to impress the neighbours. As I thought, the garden, even in winter drabness and with the grass close to the house churned by fire appliances, was well designed and beautifully kept.

It certainly impressed Henry, even though he had seen it before. 'It should definitely be rebuilt,' he said.

'But not while she continues to live with either of us,' I suggested.

'Exactly. In any case, it's a ridiculously large house

for a woman on her own, unless she does a vast amount of entertaining. She must have rattled around in it like a pea on a drum. She should pocket the insurance and sell the plot and the house as it stands.'

'Easy to say but not so easy to accept if it's been your home for years.'

We left the warm car and got out into a chill breeze. The sunlight was thin, filtered through high cloud. We walked round the house but there was little to be learned. The heating-oil tank stood well back from the house and seemed undamaged. According to the gauge it was still half full. Within the stone walls the rest of the structure had come down, the weight of the slated roof bringing down the floors below, and the timbers had burned until the fire brigade hoses had done their bit. The kitchen had been buried. We could guess its location from the outline of the house and the position of the back door, and our guess was confirmed by the twisted remains of a cooker, the central-heating boiler and other, unidentifiable, equipment. I thought that I could detect the faint smell of petrol that must have sown the first suspicions in the mind of the Fire Investigator. The whole place had been too soaked with water, trampled and driven over, and then picked through by the investigators to have any story left to tell us. The shell was filled knee-deep with a jumble of largely consumed timbers and sudden sad fragments of household goods, some of it still heaped into mounds by the process of sifting. Only one thing was clear – there could be no contents left worth salvaging.

'There'd be no point in duplicating work already done,' Henry said. 'After finding a dead body, they'll have carried out a thorough search of the immediate surroundings. We'll have to wait and see what information Evelyn Hill can dig out of them. What next?'

'Witnesses,' I said. I looked around to orient myself. 'The farm buildings should be over that way,' I said, pointing. 'Let's have a look from here. Then we can decide whether to take the car.'

The trees had been thinned to allow a view from the front of the house. Elsewhere, they formed an opaque privacy screen and a protection against the wind coming in off the North Sea. A path led in the direction away from the village, cutting between two lawns and beds of neatly pruned rose bushes. Beyond a shrubbery we were into a narrow strip of mixed woodland. The path finished at a gate, recently renewed in what looked like teak, superior by far to any gate that any farmer would have contemplated. Beyond, the walker would have to pick his or her way along the edge of a field of winter barley. As we appeared, a small party of geese got up in alarm and made off towards the Tay.

The farm buildings stood on a rise, three fields away. I could see a figure at work in one of the fields. 'Shall we hoof it or take the car?' I asked.

Henry looked at the damp ground. 'The going looks sticky,' he said. 'Let's do it the easy way. Then we'll have the car with us if he suggests a visit to somebody else.'

We retraced our steps back to the car and I drove round to the farm road. The figure in the field resolved itself into the stout figure of Mr McRodgers, the farmer. I had met him at a wedding anniversary party thrown by the local seed merchant, a dedicated spaniel enthusiast. McRodgers, I recalled, was unusual for the neighbourhood in having a South Coast accent despite his Scots name. The explanation was simple. He had been displaced from his Kent farm by the approaches to the Channel Tunnel. His compensation for the compulsory purchase had enabled him to return to the land of his grandfather and buy a bigger and better farm in north-east Fife, at the same time putting away a substantial sum in unit trusts. Wealth plus command over the beasts of the field and at least some of the forces of nature can lead a farmer into becoming self-opinionated to the point of arrogance and McRodgers had fallen into that trap.

He was attending to a bird-scarer, one of several scattered around his fields. I stopped the car as near to him as I could. Henry and I got out. McRodgers walked to meet us and we spoke over a fence of sheep-netting topped with barbed wire. He was a fit-looking man in his forties but distinctly overweight. Nature had not given him a nose suited for looking down at those he suspected of being less well-heeled than himself, but he had a habit of looking down it anyway.

Our conversation was punctuated by the bangs and hoots of the bird-scaring devices, powered by bottled gas and car batteries. I noticed that the geese, as usual, had become accustomed to the sounds and paid them little attention except to avoid their immediate vicinities much as pedestrians will cross the road to avoid the nuisance of a road-drill.

I reminded McRodgers of our previous contact, introduced him to Henry and we spent the obligatory few minutes in discussing the weather, the state of the market and the quality of the previous season's crops. The courtesies concluded, I came to the point. 'It seems that you've lost a neighbour,' I suggested.

'That's so. Toffee-nosed old bitch!'

'Miss Bland?' I said, startled. Nobody else had cared to speak ill of the dead.

'No, not her. It weren't her fault. Mrs Whatsit. Hill. Thinks she's better than anybody because her husband made transistors or something and left her a packet. Well, I reckon I could buy her or sell her.'

I saw one of Henry's eyebrows lift and I knew that he could have made a close estimate of Mrs Hill's fortune. 'What was the problem?' he asked.

Mr McRodgers's face darkened. 'Old Mr Jenkins, him that had the farm before me, he was pals with Lady Muck and used to let her send Miss Bland to pull vegetables out of the crop. For all the two of them could eat, a few carrots or potatoes wouldn't have bothered me if I'd been asked. But I found Miss Bland helping herself and I stopped her, waiting to be asked. And – would you believe? – the old bitch told her to go on taking them, because she had Mr Jenkins's permission.'

'It's a common delusion,' Henry said, 'that the permission outlives the giver of it. Just wishful thinking, but very much inclined to make bad blood.'

'You're right there. She'll be no loss around here, I'm telling you. I don't think she'll be back. I've a good mind to make sure of it by giving the underwriters an offer they can't refuse. I wouldn't mind rebuilding the place for myself. I've a daughter marrying soon who could take over the farmhouse. I had a damn good look and I think the stonework's still sound. I might get a surveyor to look at it. It were the kind of house a man could be proud of. Too good for the likes of her.'

I could see how Mrs Hill might have found the farmer 'mean-spirited' just as I could see how Mrs Hill had managed to get so firmly up his insignificant nose. It was a clash of temperaments and backgrounds and to pursue it might have set him off on another profit-less diatribe. Instead I asked, 'Have the police been on at you?'

He nodded solemnly. 'That they have. Wanting to know all that I'd seen on the day of the fire.'

'We'd be grateful if you'd tell it to us,' Henry said. He hesitated and then decided to lay his cards on the table. 'The police have been giving Mrs Hill a hard time and she's asked us to look into it and make sure that she gets fair treatment.'

I half expected him to tell us to go to hell, but instead he nodded. It seemed that his mistrust of insurance companies outweighed even his dislike of Mrs Hill. 'I can understand that,' the farmer said. 'One word out of place from the police and the insurance doesn't pay up. There's no doubt in my mind, they thought she'd set the fire herself, yes, and knocked the other lady over the head.' He paused and glared at the distant geese while he ruminated. 'I'd've been just as happy to see it that way, and frankly I could have believed it of her, but no. You have to tell it the way it is, and I was out here most of the day . . . trying to keep those buggers off my corn,' he added grimly,

shaking his fist as another small skein of geese spir-
alled down.

The diversion was tempting but we were not there
to further our own interests. 'How do you mean?' I
asked.

He picked me up wrongly. 'Its not what they eat,
it's the damage they do paddling around on their great
flat feet and shitting everywhere. They eat maybe a
bushel of young barley and leave a ruined field behind
them.'

'What I meant was,' I said patiently, 'what did *you*
mean about telling it the way it is?'

'Oh, that! I'd like to be able to say she came home
half an hour or an hour before I saw the fire. Maybe
she did, but if she did I didn't see her. It's lonely and
boring in the fields at this time of year. If there's no
machinery going, sound carries and you can't help
looking up at the sound of a car. Not if there's nothing
out of the ordinary about it and it's going past on the
road, maybe, but if it slows down to turn off. There
was one car before the fire and I told the police. I
didn't see it, I'd moved to where the house was hidden
by the trees, but I heard it. It started up again suddenly
after half an hour, turned quickly with a lot of loud
scuffing on the gravel.'

'Could it have been Mrs Hill's car?' I asked him.

'The police asked me that. I said you get more
difference in the sound of the same car with a change
of driver or humidity in the air than you do between
one tin box and another. For all I could tell from the
sound of it, it could have been her Audi, but from
the sound of the driving it was somebody very dif-

ferent. She drives the way an old woman butters a scone. Very fiddly and not caring how long it takes.'

'Did you hear the dog?' Henry asked keenly.

'That dog of hers had been barking but it stopped suddenly as the car went off again. Is it true that he just drove over the top of the poor bugger?'

'That's so,' I said.

'Damn shame!' Farmers have usually outgrown any sentimentality about animals but Mr McRodgers sounded genuinely indignant. 'Soon after that, I came in sight of the house again and saw smoke at the upper windows and I hurried to my house to dial nine-nine-nine. I stayed on my own ground, mind, because it was no business of mine, but I kept my eyes open. And about another twenty minutes later Lady Muck turns up. But the roof was already burning and the brigade was there by then.'

That seemed to bear out Mrs Hill's version of events. On the other hand, the earlier visitor could have been the lady herself, allowing excitement to affect her caution at the wheel, or even being driven by somebody else.

'You met Miss Bland,' Henry said. 'What did you think of her?'

The farmer hesitated and then nodded. 'I met her a time or two. It's a damn shame. Like I said, it weren't her fault about the veggies. I liked her and I'm not often wrong, not about a woman.' He laughed fatly, setting his chins wobbling, and then sobered. 'All the same, she wasn't all that she seemed.'

'Why do you say that?'

'I'll tell you. I keep my eyes open, moving about

the farm. Well, you must. There's poachers and stock-thieves and men that'll make off with any bit of tools or machinery that's left unguarded. There's fools that'll leave gates open out of ignorance or close them when you want them open. And there's other buggers that'll set fires to pay off old scores or just out of devilment. So I like to know who's hanging around. And I used to see Miss Bland go off most afternoons on her motor scooter. And two days out of three . . . Do you see that small clump of trees, the far side of the road?' We said that we did. 'Well, two days out of three, she'd hide her putt-putt in there and be picked up by a car; but if she knew that anyone could see her she'd ride past and come back a minute later. I was just a figure in the fields in the distance to her and not a person to be noticed, and I never said a word about it. Well, it was none of my business if she had a fancy man.'

'It was always the same car?' I asked.

'Well, no. I noticed two or three colours, and whether each car of one colour was the same car each time I couldn't swear to. But, all the same, I reckoned that she had a boyfriend. Maybe more than one, but that was none of my business either and I'd no need to get her into hot water with her hoity-toity boss.'

'Was Miss Bland that sort of woman?' Henry asked.

'They're all that sort, given half a chance,' said the farmer. 'And who could blame her if she saw a chance to catch a husband instead of spending her life slaving for a stuck-up harridan like that one?'

I asked, 'Was there nothing distinctive about any of the cars?'

'Not from a distance. Except . . . except once or

twice it was a big four-by-four, could have been any make and model for all I could make out at that distance, but it was bright red. You don't get many of those. It doesn't go, somehow, in the country, you more often see olive green.' He broke off to glare over my shoulder again. I did not have to look round. I could tell by the chattering as of a crowd of people at a cocktail party that a large skein of greylag geese was approaching. 'I can't stand here talking,' he said. 'Got to try and keep these buggers on the move.'

'They get used to these scarers,' I said.

'Too damn right.'

'Shooting one or two sometimes gets the message across,' I said. 'Would you like us to come back tomorrow?'

My shooting had become more or less limited to farmers' enemies and occasionally, when invited, to pheasants released months earlier with that purpose in view – which I considered to be far more humane than rearing poultry in captivity for certain and early slaughter. About wildfowl I was becoming ambivalent. I had haunted the foreshore in my time, hoping to ambush a wild goose or duck, and I relished the memory of dawns spent on the mud-flats. I still accepted the view that only a harvestable surplus was taken, a surplus which would have died in the winter anyway or failed to find breeding space in the spring; but they were no enemy of mine and I had made little contribution to their existence, so I was sparing in my forays against them. But there was no doubt that a wild goose made a very acceptable Christmas dinner and there was a special thrill to the hunt for a truly wild quarry. Beth became understandably nervous if I went out on the mud-flats alone; but decoying on farmland at the farmer's request was another matter entirely and valuable experience for the dogs.

McRodgers paused for a few seconds, as though afraid that being too eager would somehow put him in my debt. 'You'd be very welcome to come back,' he said at last. As soon as the words were out he looked for the snag. 'You won't be wanting straw bales for a hide?'

'I don't think so,' I said. 'If the wind holds where it is, they'll still be coming in over the trees at Atherton House. There's a natural hide in the ditch where the gorse is standing. If we put out a few decoys, they should swing round again and come in there.' While I spoke I was remembering one of my half-forgotten inspirations. 'You may want to try an idea of mine,' I said. 'It occurred to me, ages ago, that some insects might have the best idea. There are moths that have patterns like big eyes on their wings to scare off predators. It seems to work for them. I thought that a similar trick might keep buzzards and sparrowhawks away from the release pens.'

'Did it work?' McRodgers asked keenly.

'I only tried it for a year before we had to give that shoot up. We didn't have any losses, but we might not have had losses anyway, it was a low year for raptors. I still have some big eyes, painted on plywood, if you want to try putting them out flat on the ground. They're meant to suggest a big animal lurking in wait.'

'The crop's only a few inches high,' said the farmer doubtfully.

'I don't think that matters,' I told him. 'Birds and animals have superb senses and instincts and they learn quickly by experience, but reasoning ability is very rare.'

'That's for sure. Bring them over. I'll give them a go.'

'About Mrs Hill, Miss Bland and Atherton House, is there anyone else we should speak to?' Henry asked.

'I can't think of any,' said the farmer. 'The next-door neighbour to Atherton House is away. I know, because she left the key with me. Across the road, the houses don't start until you're over the bridge. Of course, if you want to know where Miss Bland went in the afternoons, anyone might have seen her being picked up by car, but the way she was acting I wouldn't count on it.'

In the car, I said, 'We're running out of time for the moment. Are you staying to lunch?'

'I promised to go to the factory with Evelyn Hill. I must be going soft in the head. But the place should be empty and we can snoop all we want without starting a panic. She wants to get lunch along the way. I'll meet you back here tomorrow.'

Chapter Seven

Geese are usually on the wing early in the mornings, hoping to be first on the best feeding grounds before farmers and wildfowlers are ready for them. Henry was long past the age for pre-dawn starts, even if Isobel would have allowed him to put any unnecessary strain on his heart, but he was to come and join me at a more gentlemanly hour of the morning. Faithfully promising Beth that I would wrap up warmly, take plenty to eat and drink, lift nothing heavy and use my mobile phone immediately if I felt any ill effects, I went to bed early.

For once I slept well and roused easily when the alarm clock sounded its gentle note. I managed to dress without quite waking Beth, bolted a quick breakfast, filled my flasks, dropped my packet of sandwiches into a pocket and went out into a breezy night. The darkness complicated every manoeuvre but spared me the sight of the devastated frontage and I had loaded the car the previous evening (even risking the wrath of the police and my insurers by including my Dickson Round Action) and had little to do except to fetch out a pair of spaniels in need of the experience. Sensing

great events to come, they gambolled round my feet
before hurling themselves into the tail of the car.

I reached Atherton House while the first colourless
glow of dawn was dimming the light of a waning
moon. I left the car where I had parked the previous
day. I had, as usual, a lot of gear to carry but I had
chosen my position with care. Not many yards from
the gate to the field, the boundary fence and ditch
took a curve, leaving a bulge in the otherwise straight
edge of the field. Rather than confuse the pattern for
all their machinery, successive farmers had held to a
straight line, leaving an unused crescent which was
now taken over by gorse. Wasted ground to the thrifty
farmer, to the local wildlife it would have been habitat
added to the nearby garden. It took me two trips to
fetch all my accoutrements, but by the time that the
light began to turn from grey to the colours of daylight
I was settled together with the two spaniels. Two
camouflage nets toned in with the gorse to improve
my concealment and I had a comfortable seat with my
feet in the ditch. Forty yards out in the field, a pattern
of lightweight shell decoys bobbed in the breeze and
mimicked the pattern of contentedly feeding geese.
In the distance McRodgers's bird-scarers banged and
hooted, but they were as likely to push the birds over
in my direction as to scare them away.

I waited, sipping coffee. The world began to awake.
One or two cars passed on the road. A man on a
motorcycle rode up to the farm. Mr McRodgers came
out to meet him and the two vanished into a barn. A
V-shaped skein of geese passed high overhead, ignor-
ing my siren calls. The spaniels stirred uneasily as

a rabbit, fooled by the stillness, took a look out of a hole among the gorse roots and scurried back into safety.

Then another skein approached from the direction of the Tay estuary, coming lower than the first. I blew into the wooden call which an old friend had carved for me, years earlier, while we sat over a fire drinking whisky. I was careful not to produce an alarm cry but the welcoming call of a settled goose. Several wing-beats later the leader of the skein picked out my decoys and they began to descend in a huge spiral.

They went out of my sight as they circled to approach upwind. Then I heard them coming, from behind. They emerged suddenly from above the Atherton House treetops and passed almost over me, close above the trees. I swung the gun through the leader and fired. The heavy load punched my shoulder and the goose lost its grip on the sky and began to fall. The others gabbled and swerved and began to climb. I could have had another, but the objective was not to fill the bag but rather to teach each skein that this was dangerous ground where they were not welcome, reinforcing the message of the scarers.

As the geese climbed away, my bird slanted down and then suddenly fell, stone dead. I waited a few minutes in order to be quite sure, because a wounded and angry greylag goose can put a young spaniel off retrieving wildfowl for life. Then I sent one of the dogs for a perfect retrieve. A lesson learned and a goose for the pot but, as always, a moment tinged with sadness. I smoothed the bird's plumage and laid it aside.

The day went quiet. It is often the way. After

the first skeins have left their roosts and moved to the feeding grounds, all traffic stops. Then movement begins again, at random, as small parties are disturbed off their chosen ground or decide that they can find tastier feeding somewhere else.

I heard Henry's car arrive and a few minutes later he lowered himself carefully down beside me. I showed him my bird and he made suitable admiring noises.

'Don't take more than one from any one skein,' I said. He grunted. He knew my views about restraint as well as I did and was in agreement in principle although in practice his hunter's instinct might have taken over. The male urge to gather meat, twin brother to the sex drive, remains strong in our genes.

We drank some more coffee and waited. We needed our patience. Several skeins of geese passed high overhead without paying any attention to us.

'Did you find anything wrong at the factory?' I asked.

'Have a heart. We went in on a Sunday so as to be able to collect a few documents and take printouts of what I would expect to be the vulnerable areas, which is about all we had time for, without causing a lot of fuss and flap. I'll get a look at them this evening.'

I had a suspicion that Henry had guessed more than he was ready to say aloud, but I left it at that. He would open up in his own time.

At noon, Henry scored from a skein of nearly forty geese which appeared suddenly from behind us. We drank soup and ate sandwiches. We were visited again and I took my second bird, missing behind with the first barrel – geese, being so large, are much faster than they look – but hitting squarely with the second shot.

'That's three,' I said. 'One for Isobel and you, one for us and one for Daffy. Shall we pack up now?'

'Hannah's father might appreciate one,' Henry said wistfully. It had been a lot of patience and discomfort for a single shot.

Hannah's father was a shooting man with a freezer full of pheasants, but one more goose for him would be one more party of geese warned off. 'All right.'

'But first, I need a pee.' Henry laid his gun down carefully and heaved himself to his feet.

I decided to punish him for his secretiveness. 'If they come over while you're away, I'll take one. Then we can go.'

'Don't make me hurry,' Henry said. 'Awful things happen when I try to hurry. You'll find out, some day.'

He trudged away along the ditch, past the garden gate. He returned a few minutes later. Almost immediately a lone goose responded to my calling and descended in a long curve to join the feeding flock. Henry dropped him neatly among the decoys and I gave one of the spaniels a last retrieve.

'Before we load ourselves up with gear and geese,' Henry said, 'let me show you what I saw in the ditch.'

I followed him along the edge of the field, past the gate. He pointed. In the bottom of the ditch, clearly visible where the overhanging weeds had been disturbed, there was a pile of pale fragments, some of them showing sudden splashes of colour.

We studied the heap in silence for a full minute. 'Ho-ho!' I said at last. 'I think we'll collect a few pieces.'

'They could be evidence,' Henry said.

'And whose fingerprints would you expect to be on them?'

'That's a point.'

I put my hand into the polythene bag that had held my sandwiches, picked up half a dozen of the largest pieces and then turned the bag inside out so that the pieces were enclosed in the relatively clean side of the bag. This I stowed carefully in the glove compartment of my car before we began to collect our gear and the bag.

A cat was waiting when we next returned to the car, a huge ginger beast with a very friendly disposition. Henry gave him the remains of one of his sandwiches and it was gobbled hungrily. 'Mrs Hill's cat?' I suggested. 'Or Miss Bland's?'

'I don't know. But he seems remarkably hungry if he belongs to one of the neighbours.'

'Bring him along,' I said. 'Mr McRodgers can tell us. Take him in your car if he'll settle. We don't want him eating one of those geese.'

'Or all four of them,' Henry said. 'This is one hungry cat.'

Before we drove home, we visited the farm as planned and found Mr McRodgers and one of his hands tinkering with a tractor. I thanked the farmer effusively – these small courtesies can pay dividends later – and he confirmed that the cat, now somnolent on Henry's passenger seat, had belonged to Atherton House. From the back of my car beneath the stack of decoys and dead geese I pulled out nearly a dozen plywood ovals of various sizes.

'These are the eyes I told you about,' I explained. 'I've been wondering who I could get to try them out. Just lay them flat in pairs and watch to see what happens.'

'I'll do that,' he said. He paused. It went against the grain to admit that he was beholden to anyone but in the end he added a gruff, 'Thanks!'

'I'm pleased to have them put to the test,' I told him.

Henry paused beside the cars and said, 'I expected you to ask for permission to train dogs there.'

'Too tidy,' I said. 'No wildlife to speak of. The only rabbits were in the gorse where we were. Their aunts and cousins would be inhabiting the Atherton House policies.'

Henry thought it over and nodded. 'You never mentioned those eyes to me,' he said.

'Why would I? You're not a farmer.'

'No,' he agreed. 'But, in my capacity of executor, I'm a director of a firm that makes agricultural equipment. If your idea works, we could do a deal. The firm will patent the idea, make and market the product under licence and pay you a royalty.'

'*If* it works,' I said.

I got back to Three Oaks while lunch was still on the kitchen table. I was surprised to see several new and expensive-looking suitcases beside the front door until I remembered that this was the day on which we could expect to speed the unwelcome guest along her way. When I lugged the four geese into the kitchen I could see, through the open door of the sitting room, the unwelcome guest herself in her customary position in front of the TV. There was a savoury smell coming from the oven. I went back to finish emptying the car.

Beth was arriving at the front door with Jason at heel. 'Three couples came. Two of them each booked one of Tilly's pups. What luck?' she asked me.

'Four,' I said. 'Greylags. They're in the kitchen. One each for us, Henry, Daffy and Hannah's dad.'

'I'll hang them in the barn.' In the kitchen, she felt the geese. 'Their crops are full,' she said. 'That's good. I always like to think that the condemned goose ate a hearty breakfast.'

I went out again to kennel the two spaniels. Henry, who is a slower driver than I am or who has more time to dawdle, pulled up beside my car. When he opened his car door the ginger cat jumped out. I had been wondering what sort of welcome a cat might receive in an establishment given over entirely to the breeding, rearing, training, well-being and worship of the dog, but I had vaguely assumed that Pussy would have a joyous reunion with Mrs Hill and they would go off together almost immediately, comforting one another.

Drawn by the smell of food, the cat headed straight for the front door, pacing slowly but deliberately.

Jason had other ideas. He had had little experience of cats but somewhere in his woolly brain lurked an instinct which said that cats were bad news. He planted himself firmly in the middle of the doorway and began a rumble deep in his chest. I had heard that rumble before. It usually preceded the sort of fight which was only broken up at the expense of a little bloodletting. Jason was a soft touch for most of the time, but when his territory or his dominance were disputed he did not play games.

The cat, however, had as little experience of dogs, except for the late Atilla who was presumably cat-trained. Totally unperturbed, he stalked up to Jason, between his legs and onward towards the source of the delicious smells. On the way by, I thought that he gave Jason a friendly nod, but I could have been mistaken. Jason's rumble died away and he became very interested in a dead leaf blowing in the wind, the very picture of the word 'nonplussed'.

I picked up the cat. He was, as I have said, a friendly creature and purred in my ear as I carried him into the sitting room. 'Is this yours?' I asked.

Mrs Hill looked up and used the remote control to kill the sound of the TV. If I expected the cat to be greeted with rapture and to heal the wound left by the death of Atilla, I was to be disappointed. 'It looks like one that Miss Bland brought home,' she said. 'I told her to keep it out of my way.'

'You don't want it?'

'Certainly not.'

Hearing sounds from the kitchen, the cat jumped down and headed in that direction. I left that problem to sort itself out and went out to the car again to put the dogs away. On my next trip indoors, I brought in the polythene bag of fragments. 'There's a heap of bits like this in the ditch beside your gate to the field,' I told Mrs Hill.

This time, I got much more of a reaction. She gasped and reached for the pieces. I let her pick them up. After all, her fingerprints would probably be on them anyway and there were hundreds of other fragments for the police to play with, assuming that the arsonist had been careless enough to handle them without gloves and that any fingerprints had survived several days in a damp ditch. I sat down to wait out the period of shock.

'This is a piece of one of a pair of three-handled loving cups,' she said miserably.

I knew that the products of the long defunct Wemyss pottery at nearby Kirkcaldy (not to be confused with another Kirkcaldy pottery known as Links pottery) were highly collectable. 'Valuable?' I asked.

'Yes, very. And I think this is from a pig model.'

Henry had followed me into the sitting room. He was washed and all traces of the countryside had been brushed from his tweeds. 'These are from your collection of Wemyss ware?' he asked. 'You're sure?'

'I think so.' She turned over one of the larger fragments and studied the pattern of roses painted on it. 'Yes, definitely,' she said. 'I've looked at them often enough.'

'Then we must let the police know where the rest is to be found,' said Henry. 'Will you phone your friend the Detective Inspector, John?'

I said that I supposed so.

'But . . . but why would anybody do this?' Mrs Hill demanded. 'And how could they bear to do it? I mean,

I can just understand somebody wanting something and stealing it. But this . . . this seems to be just wanton vandalism.'

'Not quite,' Henry said. 'Let's think about it. Suppose that somebody was robbing the place. He's already taken your Wemyss ware out to his vehicle. Elsie Bland decides that it's too windy to ride her scooter and comes home. She sees his face. Perhaps she even knew him. So he panics and kills her. Then, to cover up that crime, he sets fire to the house. Then he realizes that he could never sell your collection of Wemyss ware. It would be damning evidence if he were found with it, so he gets rid of it outside your property, without any delay but as totally as he can manage and he drives off, running over Atilla on the way. It was pure chance that I happened on the bits before they'd settled into the mud and been lost for ever.'

'That's very convincing,' said Mrs Hill. 'It must have been just like that. Do you think the police will accept it?'

'I think there's a chance that they will.' Henry paused and looked into the flames in the fireplace. 'On the other hand, a similar sort of story could be made up about you.'

'How could anyone possibly—?' She broke off and sighed. 'All right. You'd better tell me, so that I'll be forewarned.'

'Let's say that there was a quarrel between you and Miss Bland. Say that she found out something that you hoped to keep secret.'

Mrs Hill bridled. 'What sort of something?' she demanded.

Henry waved his arms in an overgrown shrug. 'I don't know. For me to know that, there'd have to *be* something.'

The cat, smelling strongly of fish, came back and jumped uninvited onto my lap where he settled down, purring like an electric motor. I stroked him absently. My mind was elsewhere. 'Let's suppose,' I said, 'that your collection of Wemyss ware had been acquired dishonestly—'

'Ridiculous!' she snorted.

'Perhaps. I'm just trying to dream up a theoretically possible outline. Or suppose, instead, that you'd found out something disgraceful about her.'

'That's the way your mind's been working, isn't it?' Henry said. 'It seems a little more probable than the other way around.'

'Much more,' said Mrs Hill.

'There was a fight,' I resumed. 'Accidentally or on purpose, Miss Bland got a knock over the head with a rolling pin. It could be argued that you fired the house, hoping that the death would be put down to the fire.'

'And what about the dog?' Henry asked.

'Be fair,' I said. 'In either version, the death of the dog could have been accidental.'

'All right,' he said. 'But the china?'

'Terracotta,' Mrs Hill corrected.

It was becoming more and more difficult but I made an effort. 'Your first thought could have been to cover up the killing by faking a burglary,' I suggested, 'so you carried the Wemyss ware outside. A little later you realized that there was something wrong with your faked burglary so you decided on a fire. Once the house was well alight, just as in the other theory, you realized that the Wemyss ware would be damning if it was found in your possession, so you got rid of it.'

Mrs Hill considered my outline in silence. 'I suppose,' she said at last, 'that it just possibly could have happened like that, except that I know that it didn't. Let's just hope that the police don't have your feverish imagination. And now we must go, I booked a table for two o'clock.'

As they went out to her car, Mrs Hill was still looking anxious. Henry tried to cheer her up by pointing out that much of our various theories could apply to many other possible culprits. All the same, I was later surprised to notice how close to the truth a part of one of the scenarios had come.

I phoned the police and left a message for DI Burrard.

When Henry returned to collect Isobel and they went home for their evening meal, they carried Mrs Hill with them. I think that Isobel was already regretting her rash offer. She had known the lady, years earlier, only as the female half of a friendly and socially acceptable couple. The widow, without the jollier male half, was more demanding and much less fun.

With her husband almost due back from his work offshore, Daffy was in a hurry to get home and prepare for his arrival. She crashed through the last of the work and vanished. It happened also that although Hannah had moved back into her own bedroom the very instant that Mrs Hill's luggage was out of it, she had a date with one of her many suitors. Daffy, who was slightly jealous of the less beautiful Hannah's greater popularity with the male sex, insisted that it was Hannah's flamboyant sports car that was being courted, but Beth, always quick to cut short any need-ling between the two, reminded her sharply that the fact that an earlier boyfriend had bequeathed her the car in the first place spoke volumes for Hannah's personal magnetism. 'Or something,' Beth added, spoiling the effect. She went on to point out that Daffy, now being conspicuously unavailable due to her marriage, should consider herself excluded from competition. Daffy took herself off in a huff.

The outcome was that Beth and Sam and I had the house to ourselves for our evening meal. Sam, who had been running around in the fresh air since returning from school, was sleepy and took himself off to bed early. Beth and I had become so unused to being alone together before bedtime that we were almost embarrassed, but we finished the washing-up together and took to the sitting room. Beth pushed me into one of the wide chairs and slipped into her old habit of squeezing into it with me and lifting her pretty knees over mine.

What offered to be an evening of tranquillity and other pleasures was interrupted by the arrival of another visitor. I would have ignored the sound of a vehicle and left the doorbell unanswered except that the visitor might have arrived bearing a chequebook and in search of a fully trained spaniel. Although the business might have survived on the boarding kennels alone it was the sale of trained dogs that put jam on the bread. I helped Beth to lift her weight off me and went to the door, but I was disappointed. I already had this visitor for a client. He was Jasper's owner, Irvine Hislop. On this occasion he was not seeking news of Jasper's progress nor shopping for a more biddable replacement.

'I've only just heard about the fire at Atherton House,' he said plaintively. 'It wasn't in the Edinburgh papers. You could have let me know.'

I was not prepared to stand and freeze on my own doorstep while being ticked off for some imagined omission. 'You'd better come inside,' I told him.

'I don't *want* to come inside.'

'Suit yourself,' I said. 'Be my guest. Stand there as long as you like.'

I began to close the door but he slipped through the closing gap and followed me into the sitting room. I took the chair opposite Beth. He could have had the whole settee to himself but he seemed to be too agitated to sit down. 'I want to know why I wasn't informed,' he said.

'If we thought about it at all,' I said, 'and I can't think of any reason why we should, I suppose we thought that your cousin would have let you know. If she didn't care to tell you, then that was her decision. I certainly suggested that she include it in her long list of actions to take. I seem to remember that she tried to phone you but didn't get an answer. She probably gave up.'

'That's how it was,' Beth said. 'She told me so. Won't you sit down?'

He shook his head angrily. He was a small man and dapper, with a rosy face and a definitely pear-shaped figure. I have never objected to any man dressing well; indeed, my army training favoured a certain smartness. But somehow Mr Hislop's appearance, from the shiny hair, neatly parted down the geometrical centre and echoed in his neat little moustache, down to his gleaming brogues managed, in some indefinable way, to convey an impression of self-satisfaction which had always irritated me. As with Mrs Hill, others might be at fault but in his own mind he was always blameless. Even his car was a model which managed to look pleased with itself. 'She never contacted me and I don't suppose you reminded her.'

It went quite against my principles to be rude to a client but I had had enough. I got to my feet. 'If this is all because you expect your cousin to leave you a handsome legacy, you can get out of here straight away. And take your dog with you. He's beginning to learn at last, by the way.'

Hislop had drifted into what was supposed to be a dominating position, standing lopsidedly with his back to the hearth. 'It's not about expectations,' he said peevishly, 'although when I learn that she's staying here—'

'She isn't,' Beth interrupted. 'She's gone to stay with Mr and Mrs Kitts, who are old friends of hers. Could you have accommodated her?'

He deflated visibly. 'Well, no. It's just that . . . that somebody could have told me.'

'It seems,' I said, 'that somebody did tell you. Who, by the way?'

'I had a phone call,' he said vaguely. He sighed. 'That beautiful house and all the china. I found some of it for her, did you know? I suppose the villain made off with it. I still don't know more than that the house burned and Miss Bland is dead.'

On the point of telling the whole story all over again, I found that my mind rebelled. 'I think that you should go and get your cousin to tell you all about it,' I said. 'She's only a mile or two away.' After a little persuasion, I managed to give him directions to Henry's house and coax him in the direction of his car.

He had developed a slight limp and I wondered if he was playing for sympathy. 'You've hurt your leg?' I asked.

'Just stiff. Been sitting too long. Is Jasper really making progress?'

We halted beside his smug-looking car. I was cold but we had arrived at a subject that I was more prepared to discuss. 'He's doing well, at last,' I said. 'He's still backward for his age, but it's coming. Do you want to see him perform? We could take him into the barn.'

'I'd better go and call on Evelyn. I'll come back soon. And I have a date for a formal shoot in about three weeks. Will he be ready?'

This was quite another matter. 'If you're to be a guest on a formal shoot,' I said, 'your dog won't be expected to do anything more than sit quietly beside you during each drive and maybe help with the picking-up if there's a lost runner. I'll do what I can and tell you exactly how to deal with him. If you send him for a retrieve, by the way, don't stare at him as he comes back with it. He'll think he's being glared at and drop the retrieve. That may have been part of his initial problem.'

'I'll be damned,' he said.

Back in the sitting room, I was not going to be allowed to drop the subject of Mrs Hill and Atherton House. Beth resumed her position on my knees but her intentions, I was sorry to discover, were not wholly amorous. 'Don't let's bother with the telly,' she said softly. 'Tell me everything that you and Henry found out.'

When Beth says that she wants to know 'everything', she means exactly that. I gave her a detailed account of our day and of our later discussion with Mrs Hill. She thought it over in silence, breathing softly into my ear. The cat appeared out of nowhere and, finding Beth's lap to be uppermost, took possession of it. I decided to accept the added weight without protest.

'Are we going to keep this beast?' Beth asked, beginning to stroke despite herself.

'According to Mrs H.,' I said, 'he belonged to Elsie Bland. I asked her what she called him and she said that she'd never heard anything but Cat. We can try to find any relatives that she had and see if they want him, or we could ask the SSPCA to rehome him, but I don't suppose anybody would be heartbroken if we just adopted him. How do you feel about it?'

Beth managed to sort out who was which 'he' and 'she' in my jumbled explanation, which may have been further confused because examination had revealed that Cat should properly have been referred to as 'it'. 'Leave it for now and we'll see if this particular "he" can settle in among so many dogs,' she said. 'We don't have a rodent problem, except the occasional field mouse trying for a warm refuge in midwinter, but with all the dog food stored here we're always at risk of rats. There are more rats than people in Britain now, did you know that? This beast's so friendly that he would probably buddy up with the occasional rat.' Beth had the unusual knack of being able to think logically while speaking about a completely different subject. 'What you and Henry said to Mrs Hill wouldn't stand up for long,' she continued without pause. 'Think about it. If she had done any of those things, she's the one person who had nothing to fear from the dog. She knew that a post-mortem had already been carried out on Atilla and she could have asked for the body to be incinerated – or cremated or whatever the proper term is when it's a dog.'

'But we have no evidence that what happened to the dog has anything to do with robberies or arson or . . . or murder,' I pointed out.

'Come off it,' Beth said. She kissed me on the tip of the nose. 'If you believe that a whole series of events, culminating in the dog'sbodysnatching, happened quite by chance at the same time as a murder and arson, you'll believe in the Easter Bunny. Now let's have an early night and I'll soon have you believing in Santa Claus.'

It was an offer that I never could refuse.

Chapter Eight

We felt entitled to assume that we had now seen, if not the last, at least the most of Mrs Hill. Isobel walked to Three Oaks as usual the next morning, but Henry arrived by car an hour later. Their visitor, in her new Mercedes, followed in convoy. Henry explained to me privately that the idea of being cooped up in a small house with anyone quite so self-centred was unacceptable to him, but Mrs Hill had declined to be left to her own devices or to be packed off to the shops. She sailed into the house, supremely confident of her welcome, and without making even a token offer to help with some of the constant labour, settled down in front of the television. Henry would have lingered to help, but he had claimed a fictitious appointment with his dentist in Dundee as an excuse to get out of his own house, so perforce he had to take himself off for the morning. I strongly suspected that he had gone back home.

Not more than half an hour later the police arrived, unaware that Mrs Hill no longer slept under our roof. They would have preferred that she come with them, unaccompanied, to Cupar; but she was absolutely and shrilly insistent on any interview taking place where we were and that, in Henry's absence, I should be present. My presence, in particular, seemed unwelcome but Mrs Hill, no longer calm and self-assured, showed signs of imminent panic and announced that she was not going to say a word if removed to any other venue and that she had no intention of being alone with so many threatening presences. If I were not there (presumably to lend advice and moral support if not to mop her tears and hold her hand), then, she said tearfully, she would remain dumb until joined by her solicitor and sundry other professional advisers, unspecified. These sentiments she repeated over and over, on a rising scale of hysteria until both points were conceded. (I hoped very much that she would not approach a court of law in the belief that similar tactics would succeed again. I could easily visualize a clash of wills terminating in a sentence for contempt of court.)

The police presence this time around was dominated by Detective Inspector Burrard, but he was accompanied by two sergeants. In addition to the hawk-faced Sergeant Forsyth he had brought with him a uniformed female sergeant who did nothing for the image of the local CID. I had noticed over a period of years that it was the habit of those at Inspector level or above to choose as their drivers and dogsbodies the most comely WPCs to be found. It may have been the luck of the draw but I suspected that there was a degree of rivalry between them. This might have drawn the disapproval of those concerned with political correctness but, provided that it went no further than a competition to see who could average

the highest standard of female pulchritude in his com-
panions, I could see no harm in a practice which lent
at least a modicum of relief to interviews which otherwise were usually fraught with antagonism.

Sergeant Hayes, however, although a woman and
dressed as such, had not been chosen for her feminine
charm. She was thickset with a square jaw and legs
like tree-trunks. She even sported a vestigial moustache. All questions were asked by Burrard and notes
were taken by Sergeant Forsyth, so I deduced that
WDS Hayes was along as a chaperone and in case a
sudden confession should necessitate an immediate
arrest.

I seemed to be cast in the role of host as well as
whatever function Mrs Hill had in mind for me, so I
settled us in the sitting room. We had had a number
of visits in the past from the police, sometimes friendly
but sometimes censorious, and I noticed that the note-
taker always made for the side table under the big
mirror. I placed Mrs Hill and myself on the settee
(where, as a last resort, I could clap a hand over her
mouth if she began to say too much) and let DI Burrard
and his intimidating WDS have the armchairs.

In the few seconds that were available for thought,
I considered holding our bits of news in reserve in case
they might be useful to counter whatever bombshell
Burrard intended to drop. I was in no doubt that he
had come armed with fresh discoveries. His air of
suppressed excitement was unmistakable. But on
the whole, I decided, it would be better to start
off with our cards on the table as evidence of

frankness and lack of guile on the part of Mrs Hill and her supporters.

The fragments of broken terracotta were in the drawer of the occasional table. At my request, Sergeant Forsyth brought them to Burrard. I explained our wild-fowling trip of the day before. 'These are just a few from a heap of bits that Mr Kitts found. The remainder is in the ditch between Atherton House grounds and the adjoining field. Mrs Hill is sure that they represent part or all of her valuable collection of Wemyss ware.'

'And of course,' Burrard said, 'Mrs Hill has not the faintest idea how they came to be there?'

His irony passed clean over her head. 'Not the least,' Mrs Hill said plaintively. 'I can't even begin to imagine how they came to be there or who would do such a thing.'

She was so evidently puzzled and upset that Burrard, who had been on the point of pressing her, turned aside. 'You can leave it to us,' he said. 'We'll collect the remainder and you'll get them back when we've finished with them.'

Mrs Hill shivered. 'I never want to see them again,' she said. 'If the other pieces are as small as these, they're a long way beyond repair. The idea that some-body could do such a thing . . .'

Whether she was a competent actress or had genu-inely forgotten our discussion of the previous day I could not be sure, but I did not trust her to stand up to pressure on the subject. 'I have something else for you,' I told Burrard. 'Do you know yet where Miss Bland went during the afternoons?'

Burrard glanced at his two subordinates. I read it, not as a warning but almost as an appeal for sympathy. 'No,' he said shortly.

'But you must have asked around. And only received denials and perhaps half-hidden signs of amusement or secret suspicions?'

'You could put it like that,' Burrard said stiffly. I had known him, off and on, for some years and I could tell that I had hit the mark.

'Did you ask the farmer?'

Burrard looked at Forsyth. 'I spoke to Mr McRodgers,' Forsyth said stolidly. 'I questioned him about the movements of people on the day of the fire. I didn't think to ask him what he knew of Miss Bland's activities.'

'Perhaps you should have done,' I said. 'You must know, better than anybody, that the Fifer never volunteers information, especially to the police. It seems that she was in the regular habit of leaving her scooter in a small clump of trees, within view from his fields, and being picked up by one of several different cars.'

'Strange,' Burrard commented. 'Were you aware of this?' he asked Mrs Hill.

'I had no idea,' she said. She was looking dazed.

'Can you offer any explanation?'

'None at all,' Mrs Hill said. 'Elsie Bland didn't talk much about herself but she never seemed to be a secretive sort of person. Reserved, perhaps, but I consider that a virtue in a housekeeper. I would never have encouraged her to be a chatterbox, but this makes her sound sort of . . . surreptitious and I don't know of anything that she had to be surreptitious about.'

'She would be an unusual person if she had no secrets at all,' Burrard said thoughtfully.

'I can offer one possibility,' I put in impetuously. Then I felt embarrassment. I would have asked to see the Inspector alone if I could have done so without introducing all sorts of complications.

'Let's have it, then,' Burrard snapped.

In for a penny, I thought, in for a pound. 'All right,' I said. 'I don't know anything about her manner but in appearance she was an attractive, feminine woman and still quite young. One possible explanation – and there may be many others,' I added cautiously, '– would be that her job as a housekeeper was a front for quite another sort of occupation. That would fit in with her being rather more flush with money than would have been expected, being collected by different cars each afternoon and perhaps even with her habit of always keeping her wrists and ankles covered.'

This time, Mrs Hill caught on immediately. She sat up straight. 'You mean as a prostitute?' she burst out indignantly. 'Is that what you're hinting at? Ridiculous! I would never sanction such a thing in my house.'

'It wasn't happening in your house,' I pointed out.

'Ridiculous!' she said again. 'And yet, I don't know. She never seemed really secretive and yet there was something sly about her. Sleekit,' she added more thoughtfully, translating into her native tongue for added emphasis to her volte-face. 'And there was no doubt about it, she liked the menfolk.' Now that I had put the idea into her head, her imagination was beginning to run away with her.

'*If* that really is what she was doing,' I said, 'the list of possible motives for her murder becomes limitless.'

Burrard was not to be drawn into commenting, but I had achieved my objective. He had come prepared to give Mrs Hill a hard time on subjects ranging from arson to embezzlement, but he would have to pursue and consider this new material before incurring the enmity of a lady who might still have friends in high places and could afford the best lawyers in the country. I wondered if the eventual possibility of having Mrs Hill up for living on immoral earnings might not also have entered his mind.

'You've given us a couple of new leads to follow up,' he said. 'But, before we go, I'll tell you what brought us here. If Mrs Kitts is here, it might be as well to bring her in.'

He waited, looking at me.

This might have been a ploy to get me out of the room while Mrs Hill was lured into some verbal trap; but, if so, it was a good one. I sent her a telepathic message to keep a smile on her face and her mouth shut, and hurried in search of Isobel. In this I was lucky, because she had settled at the kitchen table to update the records on her laptop computer. I had to wait while she stored her updated work, but we were back in the sitting room within a minute or two. Meanwhile, I need not have feared for Mrs Hill's discretion. I had sensed a reaction from the imposing DS

Hayes when the broken pottery was produced. Now, the Detective Sergeant and Mrs Hill had found a common interest in Wemyss ware and were enthusing over the work of the Czech Karel Necole, who had designed many of the best pieces produced during the life of that firm. DS Hayes seemed to be at least as indignant as Mrs Hill that some unspeakable vandal should have been so evil as to destroy many of his greatest works.

Isobel took my seat and I took an upright chair.

Burrard, who had been listening to the exchange raptly as if hoping to absorb some culture at second hand, seemed uncertain how to begin. 'You all had to do with the body of the dog Atilla up to the time of its burial,' he said at last.

We agreed.

'And at the time of its burial, it was complete?'

'That depends what you mean by complete,' Isobel said, obviously puzzled. 'I had carried out a post-mortem examination for Mrs Hill and removed certain samples for the attention of the forensic scientists, but I had reassembled the body and sewn it up. It was quite respectable.'

Mrs Hill showed signs of distress but I was beginning to see daylight. 'You've recovered the body?' I suggested.

'We think so,' Burrard said. 'The body of a dog, an Alsatian, was washed up in the Eden estuary, near Guardbridge. It answers the description given and there had been a long incision made and sutured.' He paused. 'The head is still missing.' He paused again. 'Somebody, presumably the probable former owner, should come to Cupar and formally identify the body.'

Mrs Hill made a mewing sound and put her head in her hands. 'I couldn't,' she said. 'I just couldn't.'

She was probably telling the truth, though not for the right reason. Owners tend to recognize their dogs by their heads and have only a vague and usually inaccurate idea of the shape and markings of the body. 'I suggest that that's your job,' I told Isobel.

'I'm afraid so,' Isobel said. She sighed. 'One headless German shepherd can be very like another, but I'd know my own handiwork anywhere. I suppose that the head must have been what he was after all along, though why he should want it I cannot imagine.'

Nobody present had any suggestion to make.

Detective Inspector Burrard addressed himself to Mrs Hill. 'You are upset,' he said. 'That's understandable. We will undoubtedly have to come back and upset you again before this is over. But for once it is possible, just possible, that we have some good news for you.' He nodded to DS Hayes, who rose and left the room.

'Good news?' Mrs Hill said. 'I can't think . . .?'

'Your car was examined in the police garage,' Burrard said.

'What was left of it,' Mrs Hill said sadly.

Burrard nodded. 'We can't bring it back,' he said. 'But when they got around to forcing open the boot, they found something.'

'Surely whatever it is would have been incinerated?'

'We don't know. There was – but here it is. You can see for yourselves.' DS Hayes returned. She put down a newspaper on the coffee table and on it placed a large square metal box, badly scorched. There was a cheap combination padlock through the hasp. 'Whatever it is was well protected. The contents are probably irrelevant to our enquiries so it hasn't yet been opened, but for form's sake you may care to open it now and sign a receipt. The padlock has been given oil. If it doesn't respond, we have a hacksaw in the car.'

Mrs Hill's eyes were popping. She put out a shaking hand. 'But that . . .' she whispered. 'I'd forgotten. I'd quite forgotten.'

'No wonder,' I said, 'with all the upsets. What is it? If it's confidential—'

'Nothing like that.' Mrs Hill was fiddling with the combination padlock. To my surprise, the little discs still turned freely. 'This is the box I always used . . .' she said. She removed the padlock and raised the lid. The box seemed to have been filled with a padding of newspapers. These were now badly charred so that I had little hope of the survival of other contents. I had forgotten that pottery has already been fired at high temperature and, provided that heat is applied evenly, suffers little damage in a fire.

Heedless of where she was scattering the ashes, Mrs Hill fumbled in the box and brought out a round object which she dusted carefully with her handkerchief. She set it gently in the middle of the coffee table. WDS Hayes drew in her breath sharply and Mrs Hill blinked away a tear. The object of their veneration turned out to be a pottery dish of pierced basketwork, ornamented at either end by a pair of flamboyant cockerels. It was not really to my taste – indeed, I thought it impractical and rather 'folksy' – but the two ladies were obviously entranced.

'I bought it the day before the fire,' Mrs Hill said, 'and I forgot to take it out of the car. I've been assuming that it had been destroyed along with the rest.'

'Is it valuable?' Burrard asked.

'Very,' said the WDS breathlessly.

'I'm happy that we've brought good news for once,' said Burrard. 'Perhaps it will form the basis for a new collection.'

Mrs Hill shook her coiffured head. 'I wouldn't have the heart to start again.'

'That's your own decision to make. Don't forget to notify your insurers,' Burrard said. He looked at Isobel. 'Mrs Kitts, you'll pay us a visit and . . . view the remains?'

'I'll come with you now,' Isobel said, 'if you'll give me transport back again. I don't drive any more.'

Mrs Hill took herself off to enjoy the unfailing therapy of shopping. For once, Beth and I and the two kennel-maids were free at the same time. We were on the point of sitting down for our usual snack lunch, helping ourselves from dishes of salad and pâté and hot crusty rolls and looking forward to a bout of unin-terrupted shop talk, when a police Range Rover returned Isobel to the door. She brought with her a whiff of what I took to be formaldehyde.

'Well?' Beth said. 'Well?'

First things came first with Isobel. She took a can of lager from the sideboard, joined us at the table and began to fill her plate. 'What?' she said.

'Was it Atilla's body?' Daffy demanded. We had kept the two girls informed of developments, largely so that they would know what not to say in the village but also because their comments are sometimes penetrating.

'Oh, that. Yes,' Isobel said absently while dabbing mustard onto her pâté and adding chopped tomato, 'no doubt about it unless Atilla's lookalike was also subjected to an identical autopsy at about the same time. And even so, the sutures look very like my handiwork. Sewing is the one thing that I do left-handed, for some reason, and always have done. That was Atilla all right. They're going to return the body to us as soon as somebody decides that there's no more to be learned from it.'

'Do we have to bury it again?' Beth asked. 'Mrs Hill's almost forgotten Atilla.'

'She'd soon remember him if we didn't accord him full honours,' Isobel pointed out. 'And the police say cremation is still out, just in case the poor beast has to be dug up yet again for no foreseeable reason.'

'Without being any more gruesome than necessary,' I said, 'because, after all, we are at lunch, tell us how the head had been taken off.'

'Neatly,' Isobel said.

As a description, that fell short. 'Surgically?' I asked. 'Knife, axe, chainsaw, cheese-wire?'

Isobel emptied her mouth and took a sip of her

lager. 'That wasn't what I'd been fetched there for and they didn't give me more than a second or two to look at it, but it was all one cut through bone and everything else and my guess would be a common hacksaw with a coarse blade in it.'

'That would make sense if he was covering his tracks,' I pointed out. 'He'd only have to throw away the blade to get rid of ninety-nine per cent of the evidence.'

Beth likes to have hold of the facts. Being puzzled makes her unhappy. 'That's begging the question,' she complained. 'Which is, why would somebody want to pinch a dog's head?'

There was silence as everybody waited for somebody else to pluck an answer out of thin air.

'Perhaps,' Hannah said at last, 'he wanted it to put in somebody else's bed for a threat. Like the Mafia,' she added in case we had not recognized the allusion.

We laughed, but at least the silence was broken. 'That's horses,' Daffy said. 'Isn't there something in Shakespeare about the toad, although it's ugly and venomous – which I don't agree – having a precious jewel in its head?'

'There was no jewel in Atilla's head, nor even a brain,' I told her. 'Did you open his head?' I asked Isobel.

She looked offended and flashed her unsuitable spectacles at me. 'Not necessary,' she snapped. 'His head had escaped the general crushing. There was some bruising under the hair as though he'd been struck down by something hard and heavy. I opened the skin at that point and my guess is that several minutes then elapsed before he was run over and killed, but I wouldn't want to be cross-examined as to how long. The skull was still whole so I didn't open it. And to save you asking, yes, I did look in his ears and mouth and up his nostrils, just in case he'd been secretly stabbed. Highly unlikely, I know, but it's always wise to be ready for whatever a desperate defence counsel throws at you. I've told the police all about it.'

There was another silence.

'Implanted microchip?' Beth suggested suddenly. 'For identification.'

'Atilla didn't have a microchip,' Isobel said. 'And no vet would implant one under the scalp.'

'He mightn't have known that,' said Beth.

'He would if he had any sense.'

Isobel was beginning to bristle at the apparent slurs on her competence. To quiet her wrath or at least turn it away from Beth, 'If we're exploring the realms of the improbable,' I said, 'he may have wanted it for a trophy to mount on his wall. There was something definitely wolflike about Atilla's head. I can't think of any other motive.'

My suggestion, facetious as it was, was scorned but nobody had anything better to offer by the time our snacks were finished, so we went about the afternoon's business. As dusk approached, I took four dogs and a gun in the car and visited a wood where wood pigeon can usually be expected to fly in to roost. The pigeon duly arrived. The dogs remained steady. Each had had prior experience of carrying wood pigeon safely contained in an old stocking-foot. The progression to picking up the still warm and loose-feathered birds was accomplished without disaster.

I returned home, pleased. Any purchaser would certainly expect his companion to be proficient at retrieving one of the most challenging quarries, but some dogs find them difficult and unpalatable. In the twilight, the damage to the house hardly showed at all. I was further pleased to note that Henry's car was in the driveway but Mrs Hill's was not. Henry was already enjoying tea in the sitting room while studying some papers. I fetched a biscuit and tea for myself and, feeling leg-weary, went to join him. 'How was the dentist?' I asked.

'I don't know. I haven't been near him. I've been at home. I wanted a chance to study Mrs Hill's papers without having her breathe impatiently down my neck and ask me every three minutes what I'd found.'

'I'll do the job for her,' I told him. 'What *have* you found?'

'Enough to start me thinking. Superficially, which is as far as I've had time to go for the moment, the accounting seems to be in order. But the Managing Director, a man called Huggett, is on several other boards of directors. It's by arrangement, Mrs Hill assures me, and the minutes suggest that he has been meticulous about declaring any conflict of interest, so there's nothing wrong with that. All the same, it made me suspicious. So I began to wonder how I'd set about conjuring money out of the firm and into my own pocket, were I so inclined. Direct removal of money in cash or by electronic transfer would be visible to too many people. I took a look at a particularly vulnerable area and then spent a little time on the phone.' Henry gave me a penetrating look over his half-glasses. 'This is in strictest confidence, mind.'

'Of course,' I said.

'And don't you think that we may be coming close to the usual hour for lubricating the thought processes with a little alcohol?'

This was a blatant demand for a bribe. I got to my feet and poured us a beer apiece.

Henry sighed. 'I had something a little stronger in mind,' he said, 'but no doubt you regard that as a carrot for the donkey. Trading advantage, in the right circumstances, can be as valuable as money in the bank. The factory is rather bigger than I expected. It's Europe's third-biggest manufacturer of circuit boards.'

'That's big,' I said obligingly.

'Yes. I took a look at their list of running contracts and found that a Kirkcaldy firm (which I'll leave nameless for the moment if you don't mind), a firm making satellite navigation equipment, is a major customer and is getting its circuit boards at a fraction of the price the others are paying. To Hill and Co. the loss would be dwarfed by the profits elsewhere but to the smaller firm the saving would be large enough to enable them to underbid their rivals.' Henry took a pull at his beer. 'Over the phone, I discovered that one of the directors, and a major shareholder, is a person by the name of Huggett.'

'Oho!' I said. 'The same name as Mrs Hill's MD.'

'Don't leap to too hasty a conclusion. The initials are different. That could be a cover-up or it could be coincidence, but I'm very much inclined to suspect that it's a relative.'

'Surely the auditor should have queried it?'

'The auditor,' Henry said slowly, 'is Mrs Hill's cousin.'

'Hislop?'

'The same. And when I made enquiries of some of my Edinburgh contacts I got the evasive silence and sudden change of subject which are as damning as faint praise. After pushing fairly hard, I discovered that he's in a small way of business, not considered very competent and mixes with a rather dubious crowd. Whether that crowd includes either of the Messrs Huggett I was unable to discover.'

I got up and poured him a whisky. He seemed to have earned it. 'Did you tell Mrs Hill about your suspicions?' I asked him as I resumed my chair.

'I haven't seen her since studying the printouts and making my phone calls. But she'll have to know. And so will the police.'

'That'll be up to her, won't it?'

Henry's expressive eyebrows shot up. 'You think so? If what I suspect has foundation, we already have a possible motive for an attempt on Mrs Hill. She may not have suspected anything, but she may quite innocently have given them reason to believe that she was on the track. Imagine the danger she might be in if it was known that she was wandering around with this information in her head.'

'You, too,' I pointed out.

'Heavens, yes!' Henry tried to sound as though he had already considered that danger and was prepared to brave it but I could tell, from his sudden perspiration and the whitening of his knuckles and around his mouth, that his own possible danger came as a shock.

Chapter Nine

Henry broke the bad news to Mrs Hill that evening. The occasion took place at Henry's house so that I was spared from being present, but I gathered from him that she took it badly, her emotions ranging from disbelief through sorrow to blazing fury. She was in full agreement that the police must be informed and was eventually persuaded that she would very soon have to make herself scarce until the fuss and flap had died down, but about one thing she was adamant. Closing her mind to the fact that her cousin had to be either incompetent or guilty, she insisted that an explanation must first be demanded of him.

In the morning she was still as determined and, after a little thought, Henry decided that there could be advantages to an early confrontation with the auditor. Rather than forewarn him, however, he brought Mrs Hill to Three Oaks and insisted that I lure Mr Hislop into coming to us by some tale about Jasper's health or progress.

As may be imagined, I was extremely reluctant to become further embroiled in Mrs Hill's complex affairs. I had work to do and a business to run. Isobel had gone off to reinforce her control of our competition hopefuls by picking-up on a commercial shoot, with Daffy as her driver and relief dog-keeper, and with those two absent the routine work of the kennels would put a burden on Beth, Hannah and me. Moreover, I was not prepared to lie to a client about the health or progress of his dog. Yielding to their combined persuasion, however, I went so far as to get Mr Hislop on the phone and assure him, quite truthfully, that Jasper had suddenly begun to make progress and that I would now like to see them working together.

The accountant expressed delight at the news. He had, he said, resigned himself to spending the remainder of the season without a dog that could be considered more than a decorative accessory, but he had been invited, by an important client, to shoot pheasants and ground game on a walked-up day in ten days' time on a shoot which he knew was very short of working dogs. Would it be possible for him to work Jasper so soon and thereby score Brownie points with his client? Jumping on the chance, I said that it might if we began an immediate joint effort.

Hislop said that he would come through as soon as he could, leaving me to wonder whether this would be now or in a week's time. Henry was understandably peevish but Mrs Hill seemed relieved to have postponed the unpleasantness. But Hislop must have left Edinburgh within minutes because he drove through the gates barely an hour later. By that time, Henry and Mrs Hill had disappeared (on a visit to DI Burrard, I discovered later). This, in a way, was just as well, because in the interim a uniformed constable, his face the very picture of distaste, had delivered a bundle containing the remains of Atilla, now rather smelly and, although wrapped, clearly recognizable from the shape as a large but headless animal. Mrs Hill (who was later reminded to wax sentimental over her late friend) would undoubtedly have lost what little cool she had ever possessed.

It seemed best to get Atilla underground again as soon as possible. Hannah and I were in the process of repeating the burial of what remained of Atilla and his mistress's by now barely recognizable coat when Hislop arrived. We were not pretending to hold a solemn funeral but nevertheless he stood by as Mrs Hill's sole representative at the obsequies. He was still as meticulously dressed as ever but had changed his polished shoes for shooting boots.

I left Hannah to tidy the grass and took Hislop round to where Jasper was kennelled, fetching the necessary tools and paraphernalia on the way. The dog gave his usual enthusiastic welcome – to me more than to his owner, I thought. I led them both out of the back gate. The adjacent field was in pasture but the cattle were elsewhere so for the moment we had full use of it.

We worked our way through the whole range of training. Hislop gave the commands while I stayed beside him, instructing him in whispers. Jasper heeled and sat and came. I gave his master a few low words of command all to himself whenever he was tempted to let Jasper off with any trace of disobedience. Jasper responded, after a fashion, to hand signals and retrieved first a feathered and then a fur-covered dummy. As a final test, I fired a dummy from the launcher. Jasper sat tight to the sound of the shot, watching the dummy land, and when Hislop released him went straight to the fall and hunted for a moment before making a successful retrieve. I had been playing for time but just when I could have welcomed an excuse for delay Jasper, in his usual way, had perversely become perfection. I was tempted to go on for a blind retrieve but decided to call a halt. If the dog became bored with repetition, anything could happen; and the dog was more important, at least to me, than the convenience of Mrs Hill and Henry.

Hislop was trying not to show it, but he was delighted. I made sure that he made a fuss of the dog and rewarded him with biscuits from my pocket.

'That's enough for the moment,' I said. 'You can take him away if you want, but if he isn't schooled regularly for the next week he'll slip back. Will you leave him with me for a little longer? It's up to you.'

'I suppose so,' he said reluctantly. I could understand his reluctance. Leaving a dog with a professional trainer is an expensive matter. I had sometimes wondered how an accountant in a small way of business could afford the bills which, to do him justice, were always settled without more than a slight delay. Now that I knew him for Mrs Hill's cousin I could guess that she was authorizing auditor's fees above the norm. She had never struck me as a generous person but perhaps she had a strong sense of family.

'Come back whenever you can,' I said, 'and we'll try him on cold birds and rabbits and then see if we can find the real thing. I can't guarantee that he'll be ready to perform in another ten days but you can give him a try. Just for God's sake put him back in the car if he gets out of hand or shows any sign of running in.'

Hislop promised faithfully to do as I said and probably he thought that he was being truthful, but I knew that he would not. Half my income came from remedying the damage done by inexperienced and impatient owners.

We returned Jasper to his kennel. When we reached the front of the house, Henry and Mrs Hill were getting out of the latter's Mercedes, to my great relief – I had been wondering how to spin out Hislop's visit any further. Henry must have impressed on Mrs Hill not to land me in the mire with a client, because she called out, in an artificial voice of surprise, 'Irvine! We were just going to phone you.' She would never have thought of that for herself.

'Yes?' Hislop nodded to Henry. The two had met before.

'Come inside, Irvine. I want a chat.'

Hislop looked at his watch. He seemed uneasy. 'I have to meet a client . . .'

'I'm a client too, and a big one. This is important. It won't take long.'

'Oh, all right.' His manner was grudging and not what I would have expected between an auditor and a major client.

The three of them went inside. I turned my attention to some of my younger pupils. I had a six-month pup on the heavy table that stands at the end of the runs and was giving him a good brushing after instilling some of the basic elements of obedience into him when Hislop came out of the house. He walked stiffly, apparently barely aware of his surroundings, but when he had fumbled his way into his car he drove off at speed.

Henry escorted Mrs Hill to her Mercedes and held the door for her. She seemed as upset as her cousin had been. She exchanged a few words with Henry and drove away more sedately. Henry headed in my direction. He was obviously intending a discussion so I led my pupil back to his kennel. Henry caught up with me there.

'That's brought the subject into the open,' Henry said with satisfaction. 'Hislop wouldn't be human if he didn't get on the phone to Huggett and others straight away, if only to find out what's going to rub off on himself. So I've sent Evelyn Hill away. Partly for her own safety,' he added, 'but mostly because I'm fed up of the woman. Three times a day, minimum, she reminds me that I was friendly with her husband, as if that obliged me to pop up like a genie out of a bottle whenever she rubs the lamp.'

'You should have told her to go to hell,' I told him, trying to pretend that that was what I would have done. 'As it is . . . where *did* you tell her to go?'

'Far enough to be safe and not much further,' Henry said. 'The police know where to get in touch with her and so do I. And that's enough for the moment.'

'Suits me,' I said. My watch told me that the morning had escaped me again with very little of practical value accomplished. We set off back towards the house. I was as disenchanted as was Henry with Mrs Hill and her demands and would have been happy to remain in blissful ignorance of her presence among the living, but I felt it incumbent on me to fill the conversational gap. 'Did you get the impression that he was part of the fiddle?'

'Difficult to be sure,' Henry said, slowing down. 'But if he's an actor he's a superlatively good one and yet his expression was an open book when his competence was called into question. Horror, indignation and incredulity. He said that he had noticed the differences in the pricing structure but it had all been included in a paper approved – on the nod – by the board and he had been assured that it arose because the contract in question was open-ended and government-funded, so that a rock-bottom price would still be profitable in the long run.'

'And is it?' I asked.

'Is it what?'

'Open-ended, government-funded and likely to be profitable in the long run.'

'I don't know yet but I'll damn soon find out. Evelyn asked him why his report to the board, as auditor, hadn't made mention of that little matter and his eyes popped and he began to make all kinds of excuses but ended up admitting that perhaps he should have brought it to the board's attention. Under pressure from both of us, he admitted that it was Huggett who gave him the assurance and that Huggett had suggested streamlining his report, including the omission of that particular item, in order to save the board's time at a meeting where several contentious matters would be brought up.'

'So you think he's an honest man?'

Henry gave a sardonic laugh. 'I don't think anything of the sort,' he said. 'From what I've heard, and from my impression this morning, I'd say that I'd trust him about as far as I could pee, which isn't as far as it used to be.' Henry fell silent and then chuckled suddenly. 'Did you hear the story about the drunk who came out of the country pub, crossed the road and unzipped himself?'

'No,' I said. Even one of Henry's stories would be better than the saga of Mrs Hill.

'A policeman came over and said, "I'm sorry, sir, but you can't pee in that ditch." "I'm not going to pee in the ditch," said the drunk, "I'm going to pee way, way over that field." No, I don't think he was a party to any fiddle that's going on within Hill and Co. I sensed that his indignation stemmed at least partly from not having been cut in on it. I suspect that at this moment, or very shortly, he'll be in touch with Huggett in the hope of getting a share in exchange for qualifying his evidence.'

'That doesn't sound good,' I said. 'He may get it.'

'But he isn't a good enough liar to get away with it, not under police interrogation. Anyway, there's not a lot I can do about it except warn the Detective Inspector. I'll scrounge a bite of lunch, if I may, and then go into Edinburgh. I have an old friend there who may be able to tell me quite a lot about Irvine Hislop.'

*

Henry's trip to Edinburgh had to be postponed. He took his usual quick nap in the sitting room and was about to set off when a large and opulent sports saloon swept up to the door. I heard an angry exchange and then Henry's voice saying, 'You'd better come inside.'

'I don't want to come inside.'

'Well, I'm damned if I'm standing out here in the cold.' The exchange was almost an echo of Irvine Hislop's first visit.

Henry led his visitor into the sitting room. I was refilling the log basket in there at the time. I tried to make my escape but the war of words began almost immediately and the two men stopped in the doorway and were too preoccupied to notice my efforts to slip past them. I remained trapped.

The newcomer was tall, somewhere in his fifties, with a 'lean and hungry look' and a harsh voice. He seemed to crackle with nervous energy and beneath it I seemed to sense the sort of moral stamina, in the form of an ability to shrug off pressure, usually seen only in successful crooks and beleaguered politicians. He had been a handsome man once, in the style that gets other men's backs up, but the passage of time had brought wrinkles and broken veins to ruin the effect and substitute an appearance of hard living. It was not difficult to guess that this was Mr Huggett. It was even easier to visualize his staff living in mortal terror of him. His suit was patterned in aggressive checks and his red tie made me think of blood.

'You are making trouble, for both of us,' he rasped. 'And I'm not going to sit still for it. You don't know who you're dealing with. I make a bad enemy. Bad!'

141

Henry was not so easily terrified. As a banker he had been accustomed to dealing with defaulting financiers. He stayed cool. 'Mrs Hill is looking into the running of the company,' he said, 'as she is perfectly entitled to do. She has asked me for impartial advice and that's what I'm giving her.'

'For a fee, no doubt.'

'As a matter of fact, no. I was a friend of her late husband and she had nobody else to turn to . . . *who she could trust.* I shall be making no charge.'

I half expected Henry's challenge to provoke an explosion, but Huggett had himself well in hand. 'If you're running to the Fraud Squad with these allegations, you're going to find yourself with a suit for slander on your hands.'

Henry sighed. 'You'll need to choose your words with more care if you hope to survive in a court of law,' he said. 'For a start, the uttering of allegations is Mrs Hill's obligation rather than mine. Secondly, Fife doesn't run to a Fraud Squad as such. It will be a matter for the Criminal Investigation Department, who can turn to the Crown Office Fraud Unit for help or advice. Thirdly, no court ever penalizes anyone for reporting suspicions to the police. It would be against the public interest.'

'Where is Mrs Hill? I want the organ-grinder.'

'I'm afraid you only get the monkey.'

Huggett was silent for a moment. I could almost see his brain evaluating Henry's words. 'If the accusations are vexatious and frivolous,' he said at last, 'a court might very well set a precedent. Just because a namesake figures in some company that we deal with, you two are stirring up a hornets' nest. Do you know what you're doing?'

'Yes,' Henry said.

'I doubt if you do. Any hint of police enquiries could start a scandal. If the firm's suppliers take fright and refuse to deal on the usual credit terms, our costs will escalate, we'll lose our competitiveness and eventually go bust. What do you think of that?'

'I have set enquiries going,' Henry said, 'and by tomorrow night I expect to know exactly the relationship between yourself and the other Huggett – who, I've already learned, is female and quite possibly your wife or other close relation. If the names turn out to be coincidental, we'll have to dig a little deeper and discover your relationship to any other board member or shareholder.'

Huggett's eyes narrowed. I prepared to go to Henry's aid if the violence surfaced, but the other man controlled himself with an effort. 'I swear to God,' he said passionately, 'that I'll do that woman a mischief if she goes on like this. And you.'

He turned away.

'Did you already try to do her a mischief?' Henry asked softly. 'Did her housekeeper die in mistake for Mrs Hill?'

'I don't know what you're talking about,' Huggett said. He left, slamming the front door with a violence that made all the windows rattle.

'Perhaps I pushed him too far too soon,' Henry said, noticing me for the first time. 'But not to worry. He won't have been expecting his little fiddle to come to light. Now he'll be wondering about filling his pockets and heading for the hills, as so many have done before him. But it takes several days to set up a satisfactory embezzlement. Tomorrow, I'll get a court order sewing up the firm's bank accounts. Now I must go.'

Good resolutions sometimes need the support of a little luck. As I left the house with the intention of joining in the routine labours, a remarkable figure was approaching – an enormously wide but short figure which appeared to glide towards me without the benefit of legs. Only as it neared me could I see, in the poor light, and also hear, that it was mounted on a very small motorized bicycle which, struggling under a great weight, had almost vanished under the folds of clothing.

The vision came to a halt beside me and the little motor was allowed to pant to a halt. The figure removed a large crash helmet to reveal a round face, complete with dewlaps and scarlet with heat. The collar-length grey hair was flattened but I thought that the face, which still bore a deep groove from the chin-strap, was possibly female. As layer upon layer of garments were opened to release the heat and not a little steam, clearly visible in the cold air, I was more sure of it and when she spoke the gender was at last confirmed.

'Whaur's Mrs Hill?' she demanded, in as thick an accent as I have ever heard.

'Not here,' I said. 'Who wants to know?'

'And wha is it as wants tae ken that?' she retorted.

I was impatient to get away and had little time for exchanging unanswered questions, but I restrained my temper and a rude answer. 'I'm the owner of this property,' I said. 'Now who are you?'

Little eyes glinted at me. Then she hopped off her machine, kicked it brutally onto its stand and began to undo more layers of clothing. I began to wonder where it was all going to end, but it seemed that the lady was still too hot. She came to a halt at a thick sweater so stretched by its contents that an acreage of corsetry was clearly visible through the mesh. 'There was a bittie in the *Herald*,' she said at last. 'Is it richt that Elsie Bland's deid?'

'It may not be right, exactly,' I said, 'but it's true.'

'Dearie me! Then I maun hae twa words wi' Mrs Hill.'

'She isn't here and she won't be back for some days.'

'Then whaur is she?'

'Somewhere private,' I said. 'She doesn't want to be disturbed.'

'Och, dash't tae hell!' She thought for a full minute. 'This is the wye o't,' she said at last. 'I'm Jeannie McBride. I've twa biggins near Dairsie. I bide in ane and the tither I let tae the simmer visitors. This last year or mair it's been let steady tae Miss Bland, exceppin when there's visitors booked. Just for efterneens, ye ken? So whaur's her man? Mebbe he'll be for carrying on the ootset.'

My interest stirred a little. 'So why don't you ask him?'

'I'll dae that. Wha is he?'

'Surely you should know that better than I do,' I suggested.

She shook her grey head. 'Na,' she said. 'See, the letting cottage is roond the end o' the wooding frae mine and the paction wis that I'd gang oot or bide inby in the efterneens. I nivver seen the feller.'

'I doubt if you ever will,' I said.

We spoke for a few more minutes without much satisfaction for either of us. She had no idea whether Miss Bland had met one or a dozen men at the cottage and the few glimpses that she had had of cars had meant nothing to her. I was unable to hold out any hope that the profitable arrangement would continue. She had evidently been snooping in the other cottage, because she was able to tell me that some of Elsie Bland's clothes and toiletries were still there. I told her that somebody would certainly come to collect them.

She puttered away down the drive at last, a dark blob balanced on a pencil-thin line of wheel, and I went inside to phone and leave a message for DI Burrard.

As I finished my call, I heard a sound outside and I looked up to see the silhouette of a small car pass the window. But when I had wrapped myself up again and made yet another exit from the front door there was only Hannah's Lotus to be seen. The visitor must have driven round to the back door. I followed round the gable of the house and found a brightly polished Fiesta tucked away round the corner, out of sight from the road or the front garden.

The driver, who was emerging from the car, started nervously when I appeared. She was a young woman in her thirties and quite the converse of Jeannie McBride. She was dressed conservatively – for the office, I judged – but her slim figure managed to express elegance in the severe garb. Her hair was black, straight but dressed with an outward turn like a bell. At first glance I thought that she was beautiful but when I looked again I saw that her features just missed the perfect conformation but had a slight cast towards a primitive strength. It suggested to me the way in which Neolithic features, rightly or wrongly, are usually depicted. The combination was not un-attractive.

'Mr Kitts?' she asked.

Not a sales rep looking for the back door, then. And, sadly, not a client. 'You've missed him,' I said. 'Can I help?'

'Has Mr Huggett got here yet?'

'He's been and gone,' I told her.

She let out a long breath. 'Thank God for that! I was terrified of him seeing me. Is Mrs Hill here?'

'I'm afraid not. Can I take a message?' She hesi-tated, so I went on, 'I do know about the present ructions in Hill and Co.'

She studied my face. I must have appeared trust-worthy because she seemed to relax. She leaned back against her car. 'I won't introduce myself just now,' she said, 'if you don't mind. Just accept that I'm one of the secretaries from Hill's. The staff are all jumpy. Wild rumours are circulating but the general consensus is that there's been some fiddling going on and that the police have been called in. Is that correct?'

'No comment,' I said.

She nodded. 'It is, then. I pleaded sickness and came here to warn Mr Kitts and Mrs Hill.' She must have seen my expression change. 'I don't mean warn them off,' she said quickly. 'Quite the reverse. All the staff are hoping desperately that it'll be the end of Mr Huggett. You don't know what he's like.'

'I don't?'

She laughed shakily. 'You can't. How do you think I found this place? I only had vague directions to where Mrs Hill was thought to be staying so I just drove around looking for a house that looked as though a bomb had hit it.'

'Mrs Hill's car caught fire in the night,' I told her.

'There you are, then. The man's a terror. He goes down all right with the workforce and the union's in his pocket, but the office staff hate him. But nobody dared say anything, or hardly anybody – fear can be stronger than hate. There's nothing much you can put your finger on, yet it's all there. Anyone stepping out of line, if they're junior, they get fired and no reference. Others . . . We knew that something was going on. The Assistant Chief Accountant tried to take a strong line but he was in a sudden and unexplained car crash. That was a month ago and he hasn't recovered consciousness, they say that he probably never will. Other staff, peaceful, well-meaning men, have suddenly got into fights in pubs and places and been beaten up and nobody ever gets caught for it. They say that there's a gang in Dundee sends hard men along whenever he needs that sort of help.'

She had been speaking more and more quickly as though the words were running away with her. Now she paused. 'You see what I'm getting at?' she asked.

'To be careful?'

'That certainly. But more. Tell Mrs Hill to go ahead with the police. The moment that Mr Huggett's out of the place, they'll be flooded, deluged, *bombarded* with information. We'll all talk. And, listen,' she said earnestly, 'the Chief Accountant isn't in it. He hasn't touched a penny. He wanted to speak up months ago but he's a widower with young children and he was too vulnerable.'

That at least told me whose secretary she was.

'It seems a lot of trouble to go to over some preferential trading,' I said.

She actually laughed. 'Is that as far as you've got? That's only the tip of the iceberg. Send the police to ask questions and we'll make them a present of the lot. What went on at the time of the last share issue was a long, long way beyond a joke.' She turned and fumbled with the car door. 'Remember now,' she said. 'Tell those two to be careful. And watch your own back.'

'I'll do that,' I said.

There was still a little light left in the short Scottish day when I made my escape from a token appearance at the eternal feeding and brushing and walking and tick-removal. Isobel, picking-up at the shoot near

Newburgh, was already preparing our next two con-
tenders for competition honours. I decided to take two
rather younger dogs to the Moss. Daffy and Isobel
were away in my car – I swore yet again that we must,
really must, acquire a van – so we walked. It was only
ten minutes across the road and a field, but the gun
and bag that I was carrying made the two barbed-wire
fences into annoying obstacles at which I had to put
the gear down beyond each one and then lift each
dog over. There are times when they have to risk a
dangerous wound from a barbed top strand. If the man
were to accompany the dog to lift it over each fence,
he might just as well collect most retrieves for himself.
The risk was part of the return paid for a more fulfil-
ling life than was given to most dogs. But safety, in
my book, came first whenever reasonably practicable.

The two youngsters were at an intermediate stage.
They had already met up with freshly shot game, but
an encounter with a wounded rabbit or game bird
might put one of them off retrieving for life. So I
crisscrossed the rough ground of the Moss with one
dog at a time at heel, the gun under my arm and
working the other dog to and fro through the thin
winter cover while using the dummy-launcher to give
an occasional combination of the sound of a shot and
the sight of a falling quarry. Each dog sat to the sound
of the shot and to the bolting of the few rabbits that
we disturbed, and performed a couple of successful
retrieves. I was well enough pleased.

The sun was already low in the sky when we came
back to the pond, too small to be called a loch. Here,
a large oak had fallen some years earlier. The smaller

limbs had been removed for firewood by the thriftier villagers but the great trunk still lay, defying the fungi and beetles to destroy it, and offered a selection of comfortable seats to suit any direction of the wind.

I should have hurried home to help with the evening feed, but the wind had dropped and it was a placid evening with a luminous sky and clear visibility to the furthest hills. I could hear voices in the village a mile away, a plane far overhead and the conversation of geese as they headed for their roost on the Tay. I took a seat, settled the dogs and dropped a pair of cartridges into the chambers. Sometimes a few pigeon or even an errant duck would visit the pond. I might be able to take training one step further.

The aeroplane's drone faded away. The voices of geese and men fell silent. In that immortal quiet I could hear the footsteps in the grass minutes before the dark shape of the man appeared from beyond a screen of small conifers. I had been holding the gun in readiness, just in case this might be a hard man looking for Henry on Huggett's behalf, but now I lowered the barrels, opened the gun and unloaded. Detective Inspector Burrard might, on occasions, be hostile but he was never violent.

Nor, on this occasion, was he hostile. 'They told me you were on the Moss,' he said while still ten yards away. 'I remembered that this was a favourite place of yours so I thought I'd find you here.'

'And you were correct,' I said. A brace of pigeons, high overhead, jinked at the sound of our voices and made off to find their evening drink somewhere else.

Burrard was always fastidious about his clothes. He

spread a handkerchief on the timber before taking a seat beside me. 'You and Mrs Cunningham have been helpful in the past. I'd be glad of a wee chat about this case.'

I could see where he was heading. He was hoping that I would present him with a fresh perspective on the case, which he would then present to his superiors as his own. I had no rooted objection to this – the friendship of a rising member of the CID might be useful some day. In truth, I had a vague notion nebulating somewhere at the back of my mind and if a chat with the Detective Inspector brought it to the surface he would be welcome to make use of it. But I knew him of old. Once he had what I could offer, he would thank me politely and escape without divulging anything in return. The doctrine that it is better to give than to receive does not apply to the police and information. And I was getting tired of being treated one day as a member of the subservient public and the next as a friend and informant.

'You've changed your tune, haven't you?' I said.

He knew exactly what I meant and he was ready for me. 'I have to abide by the rules and procedures when I'm on a formal inquiry,' he said mildly. 'You're not holding that against me, are you?'

'I suppose you have to do your duty.' I tried to sound as though his duty was to drive the corporation dustcart. 'Tell me,' I said, 'what have you found out about Miss Bland's secret life? Anything?'

He kept a straight face but something in his attitude or his breathing told me that he was amused, either because he recognized my gambit or at the forthcoming topic. 'We've found out quite a lot,' he said. 'You thought that she might be on the game and, because she kept her wrists and ankles covered, you deduced that she allowed her clients bondage privileges?'

'I did wonder,' I admitted.

'You were letting your feverish imagination run away with you and you owe the lady's ghost a profound apology,' he told me. 'It seems that she was sensitive about her thick joints – thickness which the pathologist remarked on. She had a lover, who came to us of his own accord as soon as he got the news. But he spoke in confidence, because he's a married man.'

I was not going to let him score off me quite so heavily. 'And I can guess who was taking her to Jeannie McBride's cottage near Dairsie,' I said.

That startled him out of his complacency. 'Never!' he exclaimed.

'It was the variety of cars that made me think that she might be a tart,' I said. 'The alternative explanation in my mind was a car salesman or garage proprietor.' Burrard twitched and I knew that I had scored. 'Hugh Morris is a garage proprietor. I've dealt with him and shot with him for years. I've bought cars from him and he's bought dogs from me. But for the last year or two you could hardly ever find him in the showroom during the afternoons – he was always doing a test drive or showing a car to a potential client or some such errand. Add to that the facts that his wife's a dragon, that he only married her for the money to start the business and that his own vehicle's a red four-by-four and there's not a jury in the world would come to a different conclusion.'

Burrard was shushing me as though the bushes had ears. 'I'm not saying whether you're right or wrong,' he said, 'but I'll thank you not to repeat any such speculations in other company. The gentleman, whoever he is, came to us of his own accord and spoke to us in confidence, subject only to the facts not being relevant to the case.'

'I shan't say a word,' I said. 'Except,' I added out of mischief, 'for pulling Hugh's leg next time I see him. I wonder where his love nest is.'

Burrard tensed up and then relaxed. 'It's my leg that you're pulling,' he said. 'At least, I hope it is. If not . . .'

'You'll have me breathalysed twice a day,' I finished for him. 'Of course. I've come to expect that sort of threat.'

He fell silent. I think that he was counting up to ten. 'I sought you out,' he said at last, 'to find out what you can tell me about this allegation of fraud. It has fetched up with a colleague who specializes in such matters. Unfortunately he is a man – and if you ever quote me on this I shall deny it – a man who *aye gangs his ain gate*. It seems to me that any allegation of fraud in Mrs Hill's factory could be highly relevant to my investigation; but he disagrees and getting any information out of him is like pulling teeth.'

'I know just what you mean,' I said. 'Tell me, have Forensics turned up anything on the fibres in the dog's teeth?'

He missed my dig entirely. 'A common sort of

worsted material. It may be useful evidence once we have our man, but it's no use as a lead. And that's all the information I'm prepared to divulge for the moment. In fact, it's damn near all the information I've got, what with my colleague playing his cards so close to his chest. So I'm driven to seeking information elsewhere,' he said. 'I can't reach Mrs Hill. And Mr Kitts has vanished for the moment. So I've come to you to ask, off the record,' his voice broke, 'just what the *hell*'s going on.'

If the matter was already in the hands of the police there was no reason why I should remain silent. I gave Burrard a full account of what I had learned from Henry. 'That much, your colleague will know by now. But here's something new that you'll have and he probably won't.'

Even in the waning light I could see the gleam in his eyes. I went on to recount, almost word for word, the information that I had been given by my mysterious lady visitor.

'But this puts a new perspective on the whole case,' he said. 'If she's telling the truth, which seems likely, and if you're reporting her accurately, which has been known to occur, we have a coherent story. A ruthless man, milking the firm and intimidating his staff. Something leads him to believe that Mrs Hill is on to him and is about to call us in, so he begins a campaign to terrorize her. The death of Miss Bland may even have been an attempt on her life which found the wrong victim. Her house and car were burnt in case they contained incriminating papers.' From the elation in his voice I could tell that he was selling himself this new theory.

'It looks tempting,' I said, 'but on the whole I'm inclined to agree with your colleague.'

'You are? Tell me why.'

'You seem to be confusing cause and effect. Mrs Hill only asked Henry to help her to check up on things at the factory after she became a little less trusting on account of the attacks apparently aimed at her. I suppose there's a faint possibility that she gave a false impression of being suspicious some time earlier, but that would be stretching coincidence. The last thing that any fraudsters would have wanted would have been to stir up her suspicions, as has happened. And you haven't even begun to explain the theft of the dog's body.'

'I see that,' he said, after a pause for thought. 'Perhaps she's going to receive the head through the post with a threatening message.'

' "Next time it will be you"? Leaving it rather late, aren't they?'

'Maybe. I need to know more. When might I get hold of Mr Kitts?'

'He's a bit unpredictable at the moment, but I'll try to find out for you. Phone me in the morning.'

'I'll do that. And . . . I'm obliged to you. I shan't forget.'

We had lowered our voices. It was only when we moved to get up that a pair of mallard, which must have dropped in quietly, sprang from the water with furious quacking and vanished against the sky. I realized that the daylight had died while we spoke.

The lights at Three Oaks shone yellow under the navy blue sky and I was cold and looking forward to my own fireside and a stiff drink. Anyway, my suppositions were still much too vague to express to Burrard without danger of his rubbing my nose in my suggestion about Miss Bland as a Lady of the Night but in her afternoons.

Burrard's unmarked Rover was parked near the gates to Three Oaks. We walked there together but in silence, each busy with his own thoughts.

Chapter Ten

When a number of brood bitches live, work and feed together, their seasons tend to become synchronized, concentrating the extra workload at the kennels into two periods a year. An exception was Hebe. Always a nonconformist, in some ways Hebe was a nuisance. But she had been a brilliant worker. Not only was she a Field Trial Champion in her own right but two of her earliest progeny had already attained the same status.

Hebe was due to produce what would be her last litter before being spayed. She would then be sold to a good home where she could potter away her retirement as companion to some fortunate but unhurried rough-shooter. Among her eccentricities was the habit of never giving warning that whelping was imminent but to start and complete the process suddenly and in her own time. We had all got into the habit of looking into the whelping kennel whenever we passed that way; and Hebe never whelped silently, so nights were taken care of by Sam's old baby alarm with extended wiring to Hannah's room. The only respect in which Hebe conformed to general custom was in producing her pups in the small hours of the morning.

After my conversation with Detective Inspector Burrard, my mind was overactive. I slept lightly that night and was suddenly wide awake. We slept with the curtains open and moonlight was invading the room. Somebody – Hannah – was in the doorway.

'You'd better come,' she whispered.

Before I could ask any questions I heard her scampering downstairs. I dragged on some warm clothes and followed. I found her in the hall.

'Hebe?' I enquired. One word seemed to cover the whole subject, but it was an important subject. Hebe was the star of our brood bitches and one last good litter would improve our prospects for generations ahead.

'Yes, but that isn't why I called you. There's somebody messing about in the garden, near Atilla's grave. But I think he heard me.'

'Then we'd better move quickly.'

'Here.' Hannah snatched two stout walking sticks from the hallstand and pushed one of them into my hand.

I eased open the front door. All the house doors opened onto areas of gravel and I doubted whether we could move in silence, but there was a sharp frost which seemed to have cemented the little stones in place. I slunk along the wall of the house. Hannah was following me closely. I nearly sent her back for her own safety, but I knew from experience the folly of tackling intruders without at least one honest witness to hand. Many a burglar has made more from suing an irate householder than he ever made from his robberies.

Any hope that the visitor might already have left was scotched by a sound from beyond the gable. Anger at this evidence of an intruder into my domain overcame caution and I stepped round the corner.

I seemed to have forgotten all the lessons of my army career. I was coming out of bright moonlight into the black shadow of the gable and I must have stood out, black against silver, the embodiment of threat.

Still doped with sleep, I was slow to recognize a rushing movement in the darkness, across the grass. When I picked out the flying figure, it was already almost too late. Against the sky, something large was swinging at me and I brought the stick up just in time to parry a slash at my head. In the next instant a body collided with mine, slamming me back against the wall of the house.

In falling, I knocked Hannah off her feet. The figure towered above me against moonlit cloud, tall as the sky itself and black as the Angel of Death. His movements were jerky and uncoordinated. They spoke to me of panic but were no less lethal for that. I tried to lift my stick but I had landed on top of it. He swung his weapon again. I thought that it was a spade. He aimed to take my head clean off my shoulders – just as Atilla's had been severed, I thought during that frozen instant. I pushed with one hand and managed to roll aside but he caught me a glancing blow at the edge of the hairline. I heard the spade strike the house wall but whether the sparks were real or in my head I never knew.

He swung the spade again. I saw it in double vision which made it twice as awesome. I knew that death was coming. But Hannah was still there and Hannah had her stick in her hand. She lashed out. Her blow took my assailant across the buttocks, which was as high as she could reach. It was enough. He gave a falsetto cry of pain, reeled away from us and ran, limping, towards the gate. As Hannah helped me to my feet we heard the sound of a car starting up in the road.

'Lean on me,' Hannah said. I nearly rejected the offer, but I found that I was unsteady on my feet and blood was running into my eyes. I let her lead me into the kitchen. I leant over the sink and watched my blood dribble down the drain.

'I'll call an ambulance,' Hannah said.

'No, don't do that.' I was mopping away the blood with a paper towel. 'Look. It's almost stopped.'

'The police, then.'

That seemed a good idea. 'All right,' I told her.

Beth chose that moment to arrive in the kitchen doorway, dressing-gowned, tousled and looking adorable. 'What's going on?' she asked. 'Oh my God!' she added after one look at me.

'Somebody was messing around in the garden and he hit Mr Cunningham,' Hannah said. 'I'm just calling the police.'

'And an ambulance,' Beth said.

'No ambulance. I'm not going back to any hospitals.'

Beth knew my intense dislike of hospitals. I had seen the inside of too many in my life and had found them to be another hotbed of little Hitlers. She came over and took a close look at my scalp. Her first impulse to get in a tizzy had passed and she became intensely practical. 'You'll have to have stitches or there'll be an awful scar. There's a sort of flap.'

She put out a hand. I thought that she was going to lift it and look to see what was underneath. I reared back. 'Don't touch,' I yelped.

She actually laughed. 'I'm not going to touch. I was just going to draw some of your hair out of the wound. What did he hit you with?'

'A spade, I think.'

Hannah, who had just hung up after a competently terse report to the police dispatcher, said, 'Definitely a spade.'

'Probably covered with earth,' Beth said. 'Anthrax all over it, I suppose. I'm going to call Dr Easton.'

That seemed a good idea. Jack Easton had taken over the practice of the older GP. He was a keen shooting man but he was new to the district and not well enough heeled to join a driven syndicate. He had put in a lot of time on my lingering indisposition and I had responded by taking him rough-shooting and introducing him to the area's many opportunities for wildfowling. He would not object more than a little to being hauled out of bed.

Beth had cleaned me up a little, put a pad of kitchen tissues over the wound and tied it in place with a clean dish-towel. She tried to push me into a wooden chair but I moved to one of the basket chairs from which I could reach the phone. When Hannah had gained a grudging promise from Jack Easton that he would be along shortly, I took the phone and keyed a number from memory. At the other end, another phone rang and rang. Nothing conclusive about that. A man might well not be in his own bed.

'Now,' said Beth, 'will somebody please tell me what happened?'

'It was Hebe,' Hannah explained. 'She had four dogs and three bitches, all alive and feeding. She started in the middle of the night—'

'They usually do. I think it's so that in the wild they can avoid night-time predators,' I told her, not realizing that, with the important matter dealt with, she had already changed the subject. 'Do you mind being the waker-upper?'

'Of course not. And I've finished about Hebe, more or less. I had the cordless phone with me and I waited with her, just in case she had any difficulty and I had to call Mrs Kitts.'

'You couldn't have called Isobel,' Beth said. 'Henry sent a hired car last night, to take her to Edinburgh. He was worried about her staying alone while he's doing whatever it is he's doing. But go on.' Beth was perched against the dining table. Hannah had taken the other basket chair.

'It didn't matter because it all went smoothly. I sat with her, dozing in the chair with the lights off, just in case. And I was just ready to come away when I looked out of the window. You can see past the back of the house. I saw somebody messing about at Atilla's grave, mostly by moonlight but sometimes he shone a torch. I was sort of scared.'

'I'm not surprised,' I said.

'Not *very* scared,' Hannah amended quickly. 'Just sort of nervous. I had the phone and I thought of

163

calling the police. But you know what a time they take
to respond.' We listened. There was no sound of an
approaching police car. 'So I came in to wake you. I
tried to creep, but just as I reached the back door
my foot touched something and made a noise and
suddenly, from the movement of the torch and the
slight sounds he was making, he seemed to be in a
great hurry. So I came up quickly and called you. Mr
Cunningham, what do you think he was doing?'

I had an idea in my head but it was too uncertain
to face the light of day. 'I don't know,' I said. 'And if
we go messing around in the dark we'll make it more
difficult to find out. Have you had anything to eat?'

'I had a cup of tea in the whelping shed,' she said.

I explored my own senses for a few seconds. My
vision had cleared and I was not showing any signs of
concussion. My head did not hurt too much if I
avoided thinking about it. In fact, I was hungry. 'Then
we'll all have breakfast and we'll go and take a look in
daylight. We'll have a look at the pups, too. And,
Hannah, I think you did all the right things. In particular, the whack you gave him across the bum
probably saved me from a much worse injury. Thank
you.'

Hannah lost her anxious expression and beamed.
'It was the least I could do,' she said.

An hour later we had been warmed and comforted by
a hot breakfast. Outside, a grey dawn was becoming
touched with thin colour. We had enjoyed a period of
mild weather but the forecasts had warned that this

was ending. Anyone who believes weather forecasts
will believe in the Easter Bunny, but on this occasion
the forecasters were right. The morning was bitter.

Jack Easton had arrived, grumbling, removed some
of my already thinning hair, put in a dozen neat stitches, shot me full of inoculations and left to go back
to bed. My wound was still numb from the analgesic
spray and I felt perfectly fit, but when Beth decides
that I am an invalid she becomes deaf to argument. I
was installed on the couch in the sitting room with a
fire in the grate and a rug over my knees.

With the dawn, two very young constables arrived
in a panda car. Hannah and I gave them a joint statement. Neither of us, we agreed, had been able to make
out an identifiable shape. But yes, I said, I could think
of a possible reason for the attack. At my suggestion,
one of them went out with my binoculars to make
sure, as far as was reasonably possible, that the visitor
was not still watching the house and garden.

We wrapped up well. Hannah, rather relishing her
prominent role, took it on herself to lead us round to
the lawn as though I had never seen it before.

'There!' she said proudly. 'I left it neater than that.'

It was not a scene of very obvious significance. The
stone slab was very slightly tilted, the turves around it
were less even than they might have been and there
was a sprinkling of soil scattered untidily on the grass.
I knew that Hannah, ever meticulous, would have
carried away any surplus earth and left the site fit for
a putting green.

'Shall we have a look-see?' she asked eagerly.

'I wouldn't recommend it. This has to do with

Detective Inspector Burrard's case,' I explained to the officers, 'and he may not be pleased if we spoil any evidence.'

They looked disappointed but accepted my advice.

Cat, appearing out of nowhere, settled down on the disturbed grass, purring loudly. Whether he was being companionable with his old friend or delighting in the bastard's demise I could not be certain, but he might be disturbing all sorts of evidence. I carried him back to the house and returned to lay the old tarpaulin over the whole area.

At first, Burrard proved unobtainable by phone or radio. Messages were left for him. When he phoned me he had not received any of them but was calling out of courtesy to tell me not to bother tracking down Henry. One of the constables reported our findings to him. Burrard asked to speak to me again. He sounded harassed.

'I have to go into Edinburgh,' he said. He lowered his voice. 'Between ourselves, the powers that be have decided that I'm to be kept informed about the fraud case. My colleague's laying the papers before the Crown Office Fraud Unit and I'm to go with him. Mr Kitts will be joining us. I hope that I have half as much energy, if I ever get to be his age. He's got a top firm of accountants going in as auditors with a court order and the Fraud Unit's standing to attention and saluting.' (Burrard did not know the half of Henry's hyperactivity. Mr McRodgers had phoned to say that my magic eyes were truly magical and he wanted another two dozen of them. Rather than risk McRodgers having them copied by Remploy or some such workshop, after which they would have become public property, Henry already had in hand the registration of copyright and the application for a patent.) 'It looks like an interesting day,' Burrard went on, 'but I'd have liked fine to be there when whatever-it-is is uncovered.'

'There may not have been anything added,' I pointed out. 'Maybe, even, some more's been removed.'

There was a distinct hiccup in the conversation while Burrard absorbed this idea. 'Whatever's happened,' he said, 'it's surely significant and the sooner it's known about the better. I'll send somebody to investigate and I'll come and see you as soon as I get back from Edinburgh.'

He must have issued some urgent orders, because his 'somebody' arrived within the hour. This turned out to be a civilian Scene of Crime Officer, accompanied by the tough-looking WDS Hayes. Sergeant Hayes wished to debar any of our household from observing their activities but I insisted on being present, ostensibly on the grounds that I had a right to see what was being removed from my property but in fact out of sheer nosiness. I had my own theory as to what would be found.

And I was proved correct. I took the opportunity for a quick look around while the SOCO photographed the scene and took samples from the soil and I was able to point out where a large spadeful of surplus soil had been dumped among the bushes. Then, with a certain complacency, I looked on as, with great care, he reopened the grave and uncovered a dog's severed head, very mouldy and dirty but still recognizably the missing head of Atilla.

Beth harried me back to the couch. Daffy, arriving for work, was devastated to have missed what she regarded as 'all the fun'. With such exciting events in train, nobody was going to miss out on an early coffee break. I gave the ladies a bare and sanitized account of the discoveries.

'But it doesn't make a damn bit of *sense*,' Beth protested. 'Putting the head back where it came from . . .'

'Yes, it does,' I said. It was one of my days for being maddening.

'I don't see how,' Hannah said.

I had decided to withhold any theories until I could discuss them with Burrard, but this small side issue was harmless. 'Think about it,' I said. 'A nasty person, because he (or possibly she) had either something to fear or something to gain, exhumes the dog and cuts off its head. When he's finished with it, what is he to do with it?'

'Bury it,' said Daffy.

'Bury it where? In his own garden, if he has one, it would be permanent evidence of his connection with Atilla and therefore with Miss Bland's death.'

'In the countryside, somewhere,' suggested Daffy.

'In the countryside,' I said, 'it can be very difficult to be sure that you're not observed. Also, it might be disastrous for him if it were to be dug up by some dog being walked – hundreds, literally, of human remains have been found in that way.'

'Other hundreds haven't,' Hannah said.

'Maybe, but this is a cautious individual. Also, somebody might investigate the disturbed ground. Throw it into the sea or some river? He's already tried that with the rest of the body and it came drifting ashore. Anybody finding the severed head of a dog would be sure to take it to the cops or the SSPCA and there's little doubt that the cops would make the connection. He can hardly wander into his vet's office and ask them to incinerate it. As long as he holds on to it and whatever he does with it, it's evidence of his guilt. But if he sneaks back here and buries it with the rest of the body, he knows that the earth's already disturbed, we certainly wouldn't let any other dog dig here and it's the one place where everybody's sure that Atilla's head isn't. Then, in a few years' time when the turf's all healed and the story's forgotten, some gardener or drain-layer turns up a dog's skeleton with the head detached, in a place where there used to be a kennels, and who's going to think anything of it? It was the purest bad luck for him that Hannah happened to be sitting up with Hebe. If he'd had time and light to tidy up properly, we'd never have known.'

'I see that, I think,' Beth said. 'But why would anyone have wanted – or feared – Atilla's head anyway? Don't tell me that it was the old superstition about the corpse's eyes retaining the image of the last thing it saw in life.'

'I wasn't going to tell you any such thing,' I said. *Or anything else, for the moment*, I added silently.

The builders arrived to begin the preliminary stages of remedying the fire damage. Any return of our night-time visitor was unlikely with the house almost surrounded by witnesses, so the constables were at last able to go belatedly off duty, but adding complications to a day which was filled with routine and hard work and intermittent arguments about the coming evening. Months earlier, Isobel had agreed to give a talk in Dundee to the various dog clubs and other bodies deeply concerned in the well-being of their canine friends, the subject being the health, care and general fitness of dogs. The day had crept up on us and had suddenly arrived. Isobel would be returning to Dundee by train in time for the meeting.

It went without saying that we would turn out in strength to support the speaker. Originally, the plan had been for Daffy, who was already knowledgeable about the subject, to remain in charge of Three Oaks, the dogs and Sam, but a message from Detective Inspector Burrard, to the effect that he would not be able to come and see me until some time in the evening, forced us to think again. Hannah, as the principal witness, was sure that she was the one who should trade functions with Daffy, but I wanted to show the DI the site while conveying a number of thoughts too tentative to air among my colleagues, so I insisted that I would be the one to remain at home. Beth immediately leaped to the conclusion that I would prefer the television to an evening of hard seats and discussion of subjects on which Isobel had been lecturing me for years. Where, she demanded, was my *esprit de corps?*

Rather than plead my real reason, which would have resulted in a lengthy inquisition into my most uncertain thinking, I produced an alternative reason – that the culprit, not knowing that the head had already been found and removed, might return to tidy up or to take it away again. Obviously, I said, I could not expose Hannah to more fear and possible danger.

This argument struck Beth with such force that she immediately began worrying whether I would be safe in the house alone. I was forced to promise that I would remain indoors and not open up without first identifying any caller through the fish-eye lens in the door and that I would call the police at the first sign of an uninvited arrival.

I was inclined to think of all this caution as the mere pessimism of a wife doing her imitation of a mother hen. Only when the evening meal had been taken, the others had left by car and Sam had taken to his bed with a book did it begin to dawn on me that I was alone with my responsibilities and that the visitor who had been chased away in the small hours really would almost certainly be anxious to know whether his new deposit had been discovered. Reminding myself that the early morning rather than the evening seemed to be his time for secret calls, I settled down in front of the television. I was tired after a long day and my head was throbbing.

I thought that I had relaxed but I must have been

nervous still, because when the doorbell rang I felt myself jump. Chiding myself for a Nervous Nelly, I went to the door. The outside light was not yet repaired but I took a good look through the lens before unlocking and by the light of the moon recognized the round figure of Mrs Hill on the doorstep.

I opened the door wide and let her in, quickly, before some unseen enemy could smite her down. Even so, the chill of the outside air was keen. 'Should you be here?' I asked.

'I'm being naughty,' she said coyly. 'I only meant to make a flying visit, just to collect some more of my clothes. They're a dressy lot at that hotel. But there's nobody in at the Kitts's house and I don't have a key. Is Henry here? Or Isobel?'

'I think Henry's still in Edinburgh,' I told her. 'And Isobel's giving a talk in Dundee.' There was a pause until manners forced me to add, 'You can wait here until she comes back if you like.'

Mrs Hill brushed past me, still without noticing my damaged head, and helped herself to my favourite chair, picking up the remote control and flicking the TV from channel to channel. 'There's nothing on but rubbish,' she said. 'Do you have any videos?'

I managed to keep my temper but the woman's self-satisfaction would have tried the patience of a Labrador. 'Mostly we hire them when we want them,' I said. 'But we have a tape of programmes that we didn't have time to watch. I'll put it on for you, if you like. Then I want to go out and check on the dogs.'

She bowed her head graciously. 'It can hardly be worse than this garbage,' she said. I started the videotape running. It was in the middle of a sitcom episode but she didn't seem to mind.

It occurred to me that Isobel might intend to get straight onto the train back to Edinburgh after her talk. The sooner Mrs Hill went back to her secret hideaway, the better. I phoned the hotel and left a message for Beth to get Isobel's house keys and bring them back with her. Then I wrapped up warmly and went out, locking the door behind me. The driveway was like a builder's yard. My insurers had only agreed to replace the scorched gravel with more of the same, but we had decided to pay the difference and have the drive and the gravel sweep finished with tarmac. Scaffolding had been erected for steam-cleaning the stone and repairing the blistered paintwork. Machines and materials stood around at apparent random, as if in conversational groups. We had left our cars outside on the grass verge during the day but Mrs Hill had managed to tuck her Mercedes into the end of the drive. Away to the right I could see the lights of the village while to the left the glow of Dundee lit the underside of some low cloud.

The dogs were quiet except for a little snoring. When I looked in on the pups, Hebe stirred and thumped her tail. Immediately, the puppies awoke and started to suckle and Hebe gave me a reproachful look. The night was overcast. Scattered cloud moved across the moon although at this low level there was very little wind. I had used torchlight at the kennels rather than set off a chorus of barking.

As I started back towards the house, I heard a car pass the gates and stop, perhaps fifty yards away. The driver seemed to be at pains to make the absolute minimum of engine noise and when his door closed it was with a click that would have been inaudible on a less frosty night.

Ants crawled through the hairs on my back. This had to be the expected visitor. Suddenly, he was transformed from a vague menace lurking in the shadows to a physical being who had had one try at slicing my head off and was still hostile but relatively impotent – I hoped. If my guess at his identity was correct, he was unlikely to be armed; and reason assured me that he would have no cause to be carrying petrol again. Reason also suggested that Mr Huggett must by now know that Henry was operating from Edinburgh. Reason, in fact, was offering me a great deal of wishful thinking and I hoped that I was not deluding myself.

I crossed a corner of the lawn and waited. The frontage to the road is a high wall. Elsewhere there is a barbed-wire fence backed by prickly shrubs. Anyone planning to enter surreptitiously in the dark would slip in by the gateway or have to take a long and difficult walk through the fields. There was no sign of lights from the parked car. A faint susurration resolved itself into a single set of footsteps brushing through the frosted grass on the roadside verge.

For the moment, the moon was obscured. When a dark shadow appeared in the gateway and crunched softly onto the gravel, I switched on my torch.

If I had been startled by the arrival of Mrs Hill, my surprise was nothing compared to that of the newcomer. In words that my mother had once made familiar to me, he 'nearly jumped out of his skin'.

The figure, seen head and shoulders above Mrs Hill's Mercedes, jerked and I heard his teeth click together. But he made a quick if partial recovery. There was a faint *clonk* as (I concluded and later verified) he leaned a small spade against the side of the car.

'Is that you, Cunningham?' he said shakily. 'I was on the way home ... from a meeting. Thought I'd call on the off-chance. I wanted to talk about Jasper.' He was improvising wildly.

'You'd better come inside,' I said. 'Your cousin's here.'

Unable to come up quickly with a better explanation for his presence, Irvine Hislop followed my torchlight to the front door of the house and hung his coat beside mine in the hall. He blinked at me in surprise. 'What happened to your head?'

'I had a fight with an intruder.' I opened the door to the sitting room. 'Your cousin Irvine has just arrived,' I told Mrs Hill.

She lifted the remote control and killed the video image. 'Irvine?' she said. 'I thought we'd agreed not to meet until the whole business was sorted out.'

'I didn't know that you were here,' he said. He sounded sullen. 'I wanted to discuss Jasper with Mr Cunningham.' Reluctantly, he settled carefully into the seat that I pointed out to him. 'Anyway, I don't know why we shouldn't meet. As auditor, I'm supposed to be your watchdog. Our interests are identical.'

'Mr Kitts explained all that,' Mrs Hill said vaguely.

' "Just to be safe," he said. But as long as we don't talk about the accounts, I suppose it's all right.'

'If you say so.' Hislop's manner was distrait. He seemed like a man who was trying to think of several divergent topics simultaneously. 'You're keeping well?'

'Well enough. I'm worried sick about . . . But we mustn't talk about that, though I will say that Henry Kitts is an absolute tower of strength. What did you want to see Mr Cunningham about?'

Hislop turned to me with relief. 'Yes, about Jasper. I've had another invitation, for Saturday. Could Jasper be ready by then?'

Mrs Hill returned her attention to the television and restarted the videotape. Another programme was just beginning.

Hislop must have known that what he was suggesting would have been out of the question. Jasper needed more work than I could give him in three days. But I was rather enjoying seeing his master wriggle. Hislop had caused me a great deal of distress, one way and another. 'Walked up?' I asked. 'Or driven?' I had to raise my voice above the sound of the TV.

'Er – a driven day.'

'Then you won't need him anyway,' I pointed out. 'You won't be doing any beating and there will be pickers-up to do the retrieving for you.'

'I was only hoping to get him used to working for me or sitting at a peg. Give him a retrieve or two.'

'I wouldn't recommend it. In all the hustle and bustle of a shooting day, it only takes another dog to misbehave and you've got a riot on your hands. Have patience.'

Hislop looked relieved to have managed a rational conversation and to be free to leave without, as he thought, having betrayed his real reason for coming. He prepared to struggle up out of the deep chair, but a gasp from Mrs Hill caught both our attentions.

The sitcom had been replaced by a programme that I remembered taping a week or so earlier, an edition of *Crimewatch*. The picture showed a handsome ormolu clock. But Mrs Hill stopped the picture and wound it back.

'... from a country house in the Carlisle area,' said the commentator. The first object pictured was of pottery, a basketwork piece adorned with two cockerels. Mrs Hill stopped the picture.

A great light shone on me. I now had the missing piece of the puzzle, the motive.

'You sold me that piece,' Mrs Hill said plaintively. 'And now they say it was stolen.'

Hislop turned white. There was a silence while he weighed his options. 'Yours wasn't the only one,' he said. 'There were others made.'

'Mine *is* the only one. There's a man at the Museum of Antiquities who's an expert in Wemyss ware and I checked with him. Three were made but one was known to have been broken and the other one's abroad. How do you explain that?'

'He must be wrong,' Hislop stammered. 'Or the one that went abroad came back.'

'Who did you get it from? You swore to me that it was unique. Where did you find it? How many others of the ones you brought me were stolen?' For one usually so vacuous, she was showing a remarkable firmness. She had risen from her chair and was stooping over him, halfway to violence.

Hislop ducked sideways under her bust and struggled upright with a grunt of discomfort. 'I . . . don't think that I should say any more until I've had a word with my source. I'm sure that he's honest but he may have been taken in. I'll be back in touch.'

Perhaps I should have let him go and left it to the police. But it passed through my mind that he might leave the country. I got to the door first. 'I think you should wait and explain yourself,' I said. 'Detective Inspector Burrard will be here soon.'

'But I don't understand,' said Mrs Hill. It was one of her favourite expressions. 'Did Irvine set fire to my house?'

'He did,' I assured her. 'And he killed Miss Bland because she came home suddenly and found him there.'

'And he destroyed my whole collection of Wemyss ware?' Mrs Hill left no doubt that this, in her view, was the most serious sin of all.

'Yes,' I said. 'He'd been selling you stolen pieces. When he realized that your most recent acquisition had appeared on *Crimewatch*, he knew that you would be bound to show it to somebody who had seen the programme. He broke into your house, hoping to fake a burglary, but Miss Bland came home and caught him.'

'Then what was all the business with Atilla's body?'

'I'll tell you,' I began.

Hislop had been listening with narrowed eyes, holding himself in check. He suddenly sprang into motion. 'I don't have to stand here and listen to wild accusations,' he said shakily. 'I'm going.'

He moved towards me. I pushed him back and suddenly he lost whatever cool he might ever have had. He rushed at me, head down, intending to barge or butt his way past. He should have realized that I had once been trained in unarmed combat. I could easily have diverted him into the doorpost. Instead, I brought him to a gentle halt with my forearms against his shoulders and then took him by the elbows, behind his back, and locked my arms. The back of his head was against my stomach.

Mrs Hill had been squawking in the background, but once the action turned to stalemate she seemed to calm down. I thought that she was capable of following simple instructions. Besides, I wanted to know whether the deduction I had drawn from his occasional limp was correct.

'You want to know why he stole Atilla's body and then the head? Then take his trousers down,' I told her.

'What? I shall do no such thing. I wouldn't know how.'

'You were a married woman once,' I said grimly. Hislop was stronger than he looked and he was struggling fiercely. 'Just do it,' I snapped.

Mrs Hill was in the habit of demanding leadership from menfolk to save her from troublesome thought. She fumbled with Hislop's belt. Hislop tried to kick but when his trousers went down around his ankles he was restrained.

'What do you see?' I asked her.

'Just his . . . shorts.'

'Pull them down.'

'I . . . I . .'

'*Do it!*'

Politely averting her eyes, she followed my orders. I had thought that Hislop, bent almost double, was incapacitated but he made a sudden heave which almost took me off my feet. When I had him under control again I said, 'What do you see?'

'I don't like to look.'

'*Look, damn you!*' I ground out.

'Well, really!' But she looked. 'How extraordinary!' she said. 'They look like teethmarks. And there's a bruise right across them. You should get that seen to,' she told Hislop. 'It looks nasty. It's turning septic.'

'They *are* teethmarks,' I told her. 'Atilla's teethmarks. Any competent forensic odontologist could prove that they were his. That's why all the buggering about with the body. These teethmarks place him right at the scene of murder and arson.'

In the excitement, we had not heard footsteps on the gravel; and once the culprit was inside I had not bothered to relock the front door. Detective Inspector Burrard appeared behind me. 'Is this a private orgy?' he asked. 'Or may anyone join in?'

Chapter Eleven

Little of the story remains to be told, just the tidying up of stray ends.

Mr Huggett, seeing that the game was up, was out of the country one jump ahead of the police and is assumed to be enjoying the days of wine and roses in some far-off land. A new and more honest managing director contrived to make Mrs Hill even more affluent than previously.

Our fortunes also improved as, slightly modified, my goose-repellent eyes found favour with farmers.

Irvine Hislop was less fortunate. He had been delivered straight into the hands of DI Burrard and, although he was released again on bail, his legal advisers left him no doubt that, such was the strength of evidence against him, he was undoubtedly facing a term in prison. Sensibly, as befits an accountant, he set about disposing of his wasting assets.

This was brought to our attention almost by chance. One evening, Beth and I were alone in the sitting room. Beth looked up from the back pages of a sporting magazine. 'Do you remember Sunshine?' she asked me.

The weather was still unsettled and I nearly

answered that I had quite forgotten what sunshine looked like, but then I realized that she was referring to a yellow Labrador bitch that had been boarded with us while her owners made a protracted stay abroad. After she was returned to their home a few miles away, Sunshine had taken to turning up at least once a week on our doorstep, in the hope of receiving again the care, attention and exercise which were less adequately provided at home.

'I remember her well,' I told Beth.

'You said that she was paying us the highest compliment that we could ever expect to receive. Well, here's another. It finishes with Mr Hislop's phone number. It reads – English Springer Spaniel, eighteen months, male. Excellent breeding. First-class gundog. Owner going abroad.'

'That's one way of putting it. He can't, surely he *can't* mean Jasper!'

'I think he does. And his asking price is just about what we'd charge for a really good dog.'

'The man's a crook!' I exploded.

'We know that,' Beth pointed out.

'So where's the compliment?'

'Two words. It says: *Cunningham trained.*'

It had never occurred to me that those words might ever become a useful marketing tag, but there it was and there was nothing to be done about it. For many months I was inclined to worry, because any such label attached to a dog like Jasper might well result in bad publicity or worse. But one day I met Jasper again, on a rough-shoot in Perthshire. He performed adequately if without brilliance, and his steadiness was conspicuous among the other dogs that had been trained by amateurs without the benefit of experience and a rabbit pen.

Jasper seemed to recognize me. He greeted me exuberantly and peed on my gamebag.